I0760480

Southern Graves

A MAX PORTER PARANORMAL MYSTERY

Stuart Jaffe

Southern Graves is a work of fiction. Names, characters, places, and incidents either are the product of the author's imagination or are used fictitiously, and any resemblance to any persons, living or dead, business establishments, events, or locales is entirely coincidental.

SOUTHERN GRAVES

Cover art by Katherine Perry

ISBN 13: 978-1-963517-07-1

First Edition: March, 2021
First Hardcover Edition: February, 2024

For Kenny Seay
one of the nicest people in existence
one of the greatest fans a writer could have
and he plays a mean guitar

Also by Stuart Jaffe

Max Porter Paranormal Mysteries

Southern Bound
Southern Charm
Southern Belle
Southern Gothic
Southern Haunts
Southern Curses
Southern Rites
Southern Craft
Southern Spirit
Southern Flames
Southern Fury
Southern Souls
Southern Blood
Southern Graves
Southern Dead
Southern Hexes
Southern Hart

Nathan K Thrillers

Immortal Killers
Killing Machine
The Cardinal
Yukon Massacre
The First Battle
Immortal Darkness
A Spy for Eternity
Prisoner
Desert Takedown
Lone Star Standoff
The Puppeteer
Blowback
Prime

The Ridnight Mysteries

The Water Blade
The Waters of Taladoro
Waterfire

The Parallel Society

The Infinity Caverns
Book on the Isle
Rift Angel
Lost Time
Pages of Glass
The Bold Warrior
City of Infinity

The Malja Chronicles

The Way of the Black Beast
The Way of the Sword and Gun
The Way of the Brother Gods
The Way of the Blade
The Way of the Power
The Way of the Soul

Gillian Boone novels

A Glimpse of Her Soul
Pathway to Spirit

Stand Alone Novels

After The Crash
Real Magic
Founders

Short Story Collection

10 Bits of My Brain
10 More Bits of My Brain
The Bluesman
The Marshall Drummond Case Files: Cabinet 1
The Marshall Drummond Case Files: Cabinet 2
The Marshall Drummond Case Files: Cabinet 3

Non-Fiction

How to Write Magical Words: A Writer's Companion
For more information, please visit ***www.stuartjaffe.com***

Southern Graves

Chapter 1

THE LOBBY OF Wake Forest Baptist Hospital's Neurology Department smelled of fresh paint. The place had been refurbished a few years back and still received a paint job every so often to continue the illusion of a new space. Max Porter drummed his fingers on a chair that had not yet lost all of its cushion, and his wife settled beside him. She sipped a cup of coffee and offered to share a vending bag of chips. Max couldn't eat.

The problems with his mother had begun quite a while back, but nobody recognized the changes until the last few months. Like many dangerous things, it started small. A few mornings with blurry vision. Nothing to worry about, they thought. Chalked it up to natural aging. Then, there were a couple bad spills which she blamed on clumsiness. But as both events shifted from occasional inconveniences to frequent occurrences, a dark question loomed over them all. It was finally voiced by Sandra. Took Max another week to accept it. And when he finally braved to ask his mother about the severity of her troubles, she broke into tears.

"Did the doctor say how long these tests were going to take?" Sandra asked.

Max picked at his nails. "It's nothing complicated. I think they're drawing some blood, but it's mostly having her perform basic motor functions — following the doc's finger with her eyes, walking a straight line — that kind of thing."

"Sounds like a sobriety test."

His knee bounced. "I wish they had let me go in with her."

"They would have. It was her request to be alone. You know she doesn't like to show any weakness. It's a miracle she allowed you to drive her to the hospital at all, and even then, she didn't want me in the car. Which, by the way, is a one-off thing. We are not taking separate cars every time she has to visit the hospital."

Max checked a round clock on the wall, but he didn't really see it, didn't bother to process the time. "Doesn't matter," he mumbled. "I already know the result."

"You're not a doctor. Just wait."

"I've been doing the one thing I'm good at — researching all I can about her condition."

"You don't even know what that condition is, and doom-research is not productive."

"It's not like we have a bunch of cases to work on. The symptoms are pretty clear — falling and blurry vision, she's told me that she has little pains in her neck like shocks, and sometimes her legs go numb. Isolated, they're nothing to be alarmed about. Altogether, there's not much doubt in my mind."

Sandra leaned her head on his shoulder. "I know. I've clicked on the links you sent me. I've read the material. But until the doctor says without a doubt that she has multiple sclerosis, we should not jump to any conclusions. There are countless things it could be."

"None of them good."

The lobby was large, and the nurses' counter stretched the entire length — enough to fit ten stations. Max and Sandra were the only people there. The emptiness made him feel worse. He wondered if things ever got so busy that it justified building such a large space.

He rolled his head, trying to release some of the tension from his neck, but to little avail. "I should have seen this coming. When she stopped homeschooling PB, when she said that he needed to start going to high school, I knew something was up."

"But she was right. PB's a teenager, now. He needs to be with other kids his own age. Heck, J's a teenager, too."

"We don't know that for sure."

"Honey, J is going to have his first date this weekend. He's a teenager."

"I guess."

"It's all good for them. PB is adjusting well. He wasn't ready for a public school setting when we first became the boys' guardians, but now, he's very ready. Pretty soon, I expect both boys will be dating."

Max shivered. "That's a frightening thought."

Flatscreen monitors mounted at angles off the wall displayed the local weather report — the spring rains were coming.

Max glanced over his shoulder at the nurses tapping away on their new computers. "I don't know how we're going to afford this."

"We'll figure it out. People do it all the time."

"People go bankrupt all the time, too. This isn't some expensive surgery that hits the bank balance and is done. We're going to be dealing with this for the rest of her life. And as she gets older, it's going to cost more."

"She has insurance to cover some of it, and she has money of her own, I'm sure. I mean, she's never asked us for help with her rent or anything. Plus, we'll get a case soon. We always do."

"Sure, when times are good, people will come knocking on our door. But with so many people out of work, they don't seem too interested in having us take care of their ghost problems."

Sliding up through the floor, the tall figure of Marshall Drummond appeared. The old private investigator from the 1940s tipped his Fedora as he floated closer. "Want me to go on back there and check on how she's doing?"

"Thanks," Max said. "I think we're fine just waiting."

Drummond looked to Sandra before saying anything more. "I did as you asked — kept an eye on your boys — PB is staying after school to possibly join the chess club."

"Chess club?" Sandra said.

"Yeah, I thought the same thing. But then, if I remember correctly, he likes to play with Mrs. Porter sometimes."

Max tried to hide his embarrassment. He had no idea his mother had taught PB to play chess.

Sandra said, "I suppose we should be glad he's showing any interest in socializing. I just never thought he'd gravitate toward the nerdy clubs."

"You thought he'd be a football jock?"

"No. Just something in the middle. Maybe audition for a play."

Drummond snickered. "You're talking about a kid who spent a few years homeless, taking care of himself on the streets. I doubt he's interested in bashing heads playing football or wrestling. He's had too much of the real thing simply to survive. And he doesn't seem to care about popularity or anything like that. But he's good looking enough and he's strong. Nobody's going to dare tease him for joining the Chess Club. Not more than once, anyway."

Sandra cocked her head with a smile. "We're lucky to have you, Uncle Drummond."

"Hey, hey, don't start with that *Uncle* stuff again. I allow J to call me that, and if ever PB starts to see me, I'll let him call me that, too. But you both are not given permission."

Unable to stir up a sarcastic comment, Max tapped his knee some more. "Is J home now?"

"That's sort of why I'm here."

Max could feel Sandra stiffen. "What's wrong?"

"Nothing. J's fine. Safely home. But, well, you should be prepared for this one — he's brought a ghost with him."

"A ghost?" Sandra said.

"Yeah. Old one, too. Not the age of the guy — probably died when he was barely twenty — but his clothes and all suggest he's from a long time ago."

"What does he want with J?"

Drummond clicked his tongue. "Other way around. J brought him home and asked me to let you know that this ghost is our new client."

Chapter 2

SANDRA LEFT WITH DRUMMOND to check on J while Max remained behind to take care of his mother. When she shuffled into the lobby, Mrs. Porter provided no details while dealing with the final paperwork and arranging an appointment for a return visit. She clutched Max's arm as they walked back to the car, and that small hand holding tight dropped a stone in his gut.

He wanted to ask, but her stern mouth, her trembling chin, and her long gaze told him enough. It had to be what they feared — multiple sclerosis. Just how bad, how long the doctors gave her, how many ways that would impact their lives — all those questions would be discussed eventually. For now, he figured the best he could do was stay quiet and stay close. Be there for his mother.

Leaving the hospital garage, paying for the parking, and heading onto the highway, they continued their near-monastic silence. Mrs. Porter fritted with her nails as she watched the road ahead, though Max doubted she saw much of anything. When his mind finally drifted from his current worries and turned toward the idea that J had become involved in a ghost's problems, Mrs. Porter spoke. Her soft voice boomed against the stillness. "Do you remember that trip to New York City? You were probably only ten, maybe eleven. I doubt you remember."

"Sure, I do." Max fought against the barrage of questions loaded and waiting. Instead, he let her mind go where it needed to go. "Statue of Liberty and some museums and Times Square."

"That's right. And I promised to take you to a Broadway show, too."

"We were going to see a musical, right? But that big discount ticket place was all sold out of the show. Don't recall what musical it was, though."

"Barnum. We stood outside in that long line and they were sold out and I was angry. This was to be your first Broadway show, mine too, and I had built it up the whole trip from Michigan, but I couldn't deliver. We ended up going to a little off-Broadway show. You were very upset."

"I don't remember that. Being upset, I mean."

"You knew we were supposed to see a big Broadway musical, and somehow, that wasn't going to happen. I don't know if you could see it on my face at the time or if you were just a smart enough boy — probably a little of both — but you certainly knew to keep your opinions to yourself. Anyway, we went to this other show, not the one we had planned to see — an improv comedy show — and we still had a wonderful time. Maybe a better time than we would've had in an oversized theater with a bombastic musical. You even got to meet a few of the actors afterwards because it was such a small venue. They chatted with you, made you laugh, and gave a glimpse backstage." She grew quiet. Then: "Things never work out the way we plan, but sometimes it works out for the better."

Max focused on the road, afraid that if he tried to respond, his voice would crack and his tears would flow.

When they arrived at her apartment complex, parked and walked up the stairs, headed down the hall and stopped at her door, she turned around with her bottom lip quivering. "Thank you, dear, but I'd rather be alone."

"I'm not sure that's a good idea."

His mother looked smaller than usual. Frail. But her eyes blazed with the sternness he had known his whole life. "There's nothing you can do for me right now. Go home. Take care of your family."

"You've been given bad news. I'm guessing from the look of things, really bad news. Doesn't seem like leaving you alone is right."

"Oh, nonsense. I'm an old lady and I received a terrible diagnosis, yes, but have you ever known me to be a quitter? If you're worried that I might end it all, then you don't know me too well. If anything, this makes me want to live my life all the more. Fill up the time I have left with every experience possible. Who knows? Maybe I'll go skydiving tomorrow. But I've spent the last several hours in a hospital being asked to perform little tasks like a monkey being trained for the circus. I'm tired. I'd like to have some privacy, some time alone to think."

"Mom —"

"I wasn't asking for permission. Go home. Or wherever you want to go, but not here. I'll call when I'm ready for you." Mumbling *I love you* she closed the door.

Max stood in the hallway, caught between ringing the bell and leaving. In the end, he had to respect her wishes. He went home, punishing the steering wheel as he drove, mouthing arguments, and playing out scenarios in his head. Only his mother could make him feel both proud and angry at the same time.

When he entered his small home, Max found Sandra, J, and Drummond sitting in the living room. Well, Drummond floated, but the others sat. Max had a small bookshelf built into the wall opposite the window — nothing fancy or expensive, but enough to give Drummond a new home after their office bookshelf had burned down along with their office. Max made sure that a copy of *Moby Dick* was among the first books to grace the shelves — hollowed out and containing Drummond's whiskey-filled hipflask, of course.

Sandra rushed over with a hug. "How bad is it?"

"She's not telling me. Says she wants to be alone. I don't know, I suppose I'll try talking to her again tomorrow. For now, give me something else to think about — tell me about this ghost."

"Not my tale to tell." Sandra gestured to J as she returned to their threadbare couch.

Max went to sit next to her but paused. "Is the ghost here?"

Drummond pointed to the back corner. "Right over there."

"Okay then, I'm listening." Max eyed the empty corner.

J bounded to his feet, and Max missed the first words because he couldn't help but notice how much older J looked. The once small, lanky black boy had started to fill out. Not muscular, but fuller. Taller, too. He seemed awkward in his own skin. Sandra had been right — the boy had become a teenager.

"— didn't matter where I went, everywhere I looked, I saw this guy." J paced a small circle as he spoke. Just like Max had seen Drummond do many times. Just like he had done himself, too. J went on, "A few days ago, I had enough of it. During lunchtime, we're allowed to walk around the halls a little bit, so I lured this ghost to one of the quieter sections near the library. I waited until nobody was around, and I looked right at him and demanded he tell me what the heck he wanted. That's when it all got weird."

Max looked from Sandra to Drummond. Neither one indicated they knew this much of the story. To Max, Drummond said, "What? We waited for you."

Sandra said, "J insisted."

"Oh," Max said, trying to hide the slim joy creeping onto his lips. It didn't feel right knowing his mother probably sat in a darkened apartment crying. He gestured to J. "You've got the floor. Don't keep us in suspense. What happened?"

Puffing up a little, J said, "I know you only see Drummond, but I'm like Sandra — I can see all kinds of ghosts. And like Sandra, these ghosts will sometimes talk to me. Drummond and Sandra, they've given me time to figure it out, and that's cool. But this — I don't know. And they haven't said anything to you yet — I appreciate being allowed to explain it all — but if you ask them now, they'll tell you what I'm going to tell you. That ghost in the corner — he ain't looking right. He's not pale blue like Drummond. He's almost bone white. Like he's trying to be a ghost from an old story or something."

"We know anything about that?" Max looked to the rest of his team.

Sandra said, "Just let him finish."

"At first, after I said I wanted an answer, he didn't say anything." J no longer paced but rather held still in front of Max.

"I could tell from his clothes that he was a soldier. Old soldier. And when he started talking, the words sounded like he was underwater. I mean I could hear that he was speaking, but I had to strain real hard to make out a single word. That's why he ain't talking right now. I think he knows it's not easy for us. Might not be easy for him, too."

Max looked to Drummond. "What about you? Can you talk to him?"

"I tried." Drummond shook his head at the empty corner. "Whatever's wrong with him, he can't talk like a normal ghost — even to another ghost."

J said, "Here's what I've gotten so far — he's a Confederate soldier. First thing I did was check online at different soldier uniforms through US history. I also got him to tell me that he died in 1902. That one took a long damn time. Not as long as where he's from, though. It's a town called Whitten. Or Widdin. Something like that. Last thing I got from him was the words *No bones.* I'm guessing that he can't find his bones or they're gone. He's been separated from them, and I'm pretty sure from listening to you guys over the last few years that he can't move on to whatever's after when he's not with what's left of his body. Right?"

"Sometimes that's right. What's his name?"

With an embarrassed frown, he said, "Don't know. I forgot to ask at first, and when I finally did, it was too late. He's very confused. That and how hard it is talking to each other, I'm lucky to get what I got. But it's a good start, I think."

Max paused to mull over all that had been said. It occurred to him that J not only looked different but sounded different, too. More mature.

He spotted a tremor in J's hand, and Max understood more of the situation than before. J worked hard to speak more formally. He wasn't only trying to lay out the particulars of the case, but he also tried to make a case for himself — he wanted to be involved further.

Max shook his head. "That's not a lot to go on, but I'll take it from here. We'll see what we can find out."

"I knew it." J spun away clenching his fists and stomping off a few feet. He spun back. "This is my thing. I brought it here. I ain't some naïve fool who doesn't know anything about this world you guys work in. I can see it. That's more than you can do."

"I appreciate that," Max said in as calm a voice as he could manage. It had been a long day. A hard day. And he heard more of an edge to his words than he wanted. "This isn't something to jump into lightly, though."

"I'm not. Sandra, tell him I'm not."

Sandra shifted, putting a little distance from Max. "You've had a lot on your mind. You might not have noticed, but J not only sees the ghosts, he knows about witchcraft, he's even helped on a few spells."

"I've been around for all of that." Max breathed deeply to stop the irritation he heard scratching up his throat. "But there's a far cry from helping us with an aspect of a case and getting involved as deeply as I can see he wants to be."

J said, "I've got to start somewhere."

"You don't have to start at all." Max popped to his feet. "This may seem exciting and interesting and fascinating or whatever, but it's dangerous. It's frightening. It's not something to be toyed with or explored like a game."

"I guess you all were just masters of the whole thing before you ever started. Is that it?"

Drummond forced a chuckle. "The kid's got you there. Nobody's ever prepared to deal with this stuff."

Max glowered at Drummond. "You're not helping me."

"I'm not trying to. Look at your kid. Look at him close. Any idiot can see that the more you tell him he can't do something, the more he's going to want to do it. All teenagers are like that, but with something this big, you're not even playing with fire. You got your whole hand in the furnace to begin with."

Max could feel those flames burning up his arm, reddening his face, threatening to boil over. Sandra must have seen it too because she said, "J, please understand that Max has had a very rough day. Grandma Porter is ill, and we'll talk about that later, but it's bad enough that he may not be thinking entirely clear right now. And Max, J isn't a little boy anymore. He's not an orphan on the streets anymore. He's been going to school, he's smart, and he's been involved enough with all we do that he has as good an idea as he could possibly have about what he's getting into. Besides, the Porter Agency is not run as a dictatorship. The three founding members each have an equal vote. I, for one, vote that we should give J a chance with this case. There's also the fact that this ghost client seems to insist on it. He doesn't want to let J out of his sight."

Max said, "Well, I vote no. I'm sorry J, I know that upsets you, but I think we need to look into it much further before we put your life at risk."

"Uncle Drummond?" J asked.

The old ghost took off his hat and scratched the back of his head. "It's been my experience that the best way to learn about something is to do it. In this situation, with Max and Sandra and myself being a part of it at all times, I can't think of a safer way to introduce this fine young man into our world."

Sandra said, "Then it's settled." She looked to Max. "Is this going to be a problem?"

Before he could think through his answer, Max's mouth opened. "If you're going to be a part of this, you still have your regular responsibilities, too. Tonight's a school night. Go do your homework and get to bed. Drummond, will you see this ghost out of our house? Try to get through to the guy that we're going to help him and that we don't appreciate him following our son around. And Sandra, we need to have a talk."

Without waiting for answers, Max stormed off to his bedroom.

Chapter 3

ARGUING WITH SANDRA NEVER FELT GOOD, but at least, if done right, Max usually experienced a catharsis from addressing whatever problem they faced. Unfortunately, in a house with hallways too short and walls too thin, Max and Sandra had to speak in lowered, controlled tones in order to maintain any privacy. Not ideal for a good argument.

It didn't help that Max knew he had gone too far. He had not intended to push back so hard against J — in truth, a bit of pride pulsed through him at seeing J's confidence and conviction — but that didn't change one important fact. "I'm trying to do my job as a father — protecting the boys."

"We've been through this," Sandra said, gently pressing their bedroom door shut. "You can't protect them. Not from ghosts and witches. But we can equip them to deal with reality."

"Why can't they enjoy the reality that everybody else enjoys? Most people don't go around concerned that they'll be assaulted by ancient spells. If the boys don't know about ghosts and witchcraft and all of that, then they can be in blissful ignorance like the majority of the world's population."

"Honey, that horse left the barn years ago. At least, with J. Perhaps PB could live a life not knowing about it all, but he's already seen a lot anyway. He's yet to accept it, but that day is bound to come. Probably, sooner than we think."

Max deflated on the edge of the bed. "I know. I do. I want them to be ready to deal with these things. That's part of my point — they're not ready. PB won't acknowledge any of it, and J doesn't take the danger seriously enough. To him, ghosts are all like Drummond."

"Then we have to be the ones to set him straight, but we

won't accomplish that by shutting him out of everything. Drummond can be a big help with that, too. J's really fond of him."

"I don't think Drummond is a great role model. Unless you want J drinking hard whiskey and calling every woman *doll*."

"Stop that."

"What?"

"Don't undercut one of your best friends because you don't like the situation. Drummond still tries to better himself — and he's dead, for crying out loud. Plus, have you forgotten what it's like to be a teenager? Teens don't listen to their parents. Not much, anyway. Somebody like Drummond might be the only way to get through to J."

Max rubbed his face. "I hate this."

"Nobody ever said we had to like it." Sandra lowered to her knees and rested her head on his thigh. "But think about the rest of it, too — J did really well out there presenting everything to us."

"Yeah, he did."

"He should be rewarded for that, not stymied. So please, let's help him with this case."

"We will. I will. Heck, you knew I was going to before I even stepped into the house."

She tittered. "I didn't know for certain."

"Besides, digging into some research will probably make me feel better. Let me forget about my mom for a while."

"I figured as much."

He kissed the top of her head. "There's still one thing that bothers me with all this."

"Oh?"

"Ghosts don't pay. Every single case we've ever had when a ghost hired us, they never delivered on payment."

Sandra laughed as Max grabbed his laptop. Before he could open the bedroom door, Drummond pushed through, a grim expression pulling his face down. Max's nerves fired off.

"What's wrong?" he asked.

"We got a problem with this ghost," Drummond said. "A big

problem."

The harsh look on Drummond's face forced Max back several steps until he hit the bed and sat. Sandra remained standing but only with the help of the wall.

"What happened?" she said.

Drummond removed his hat. "I should've seen it earlier, but I didn't think to look. It just never occurred to me."

"I swear," Max said, "if you don't start talking, I'll find a way to punch you."

"Sorry. The short of it is that I think — no, I know — that this ghost has attached itself to J."

"When you say *attached,* do you mean —"

"Tethered. Cursed. Look, I took the guy for a stroll outside, figured it'd be easier to get through to him when we weren't surrounded by so many of the living — that can be a thing for some ghosts. We didn't go far, but I noticed it then. His shape pulling. Not hard, not so bad as to stretch out his head or anything, but enough that I realized he was tethered to something close by. But J said they met at his school."

Sandra said, "Which would have had the ghost stretched thin if he were tethered to something in this neighborhood."

"Exactly. Only thing that makes any sense is that the ghost is connected to J."

Max grabbed his knees and forced a few slow breaths. To Sandra, he said, "You think J's been messing around with spells? Maybe he accidently cursed himself."

"I doubt it." She opened the closet door and pulled out her box of special texts — rare and powerful books on witchcraft. Not long ago, she had an entire section of shelves in their office filled with such books — grimoires of long-forgotten covens, collected essays handwritten by notable witches, and even a few spell books bound in skin. But when their last big case resulted with the office building burning to the ground, those precious books were lost. Turned to ash. Sandra had been lucky enough that three of her books were at home during the fire. "Whenever I've shown J anything to do with spells, he's given it great respect." She flipped through one book, then switched to another. "Was the tether visible?"

"Yeah," Drummond said. "I thought that a bit odd. It was like a thin fishing line. I didn't even notice it at first."

"That's a good way to describe it. My initial guess is that the ghost has been floating around, waiting for a person to come along that had enough of a gift to see him. Like he was fishing — trying to catch someone. He probably hoped anybody with the ability to see a ghost would also be able to help free him."

Max said, "And J's the first one he found?"

"Doubt it. If he's from the Civil War, then he's probably gone through several people over the decades. Maybe hoping each time to get free and failing. J's just the latest."

"None of this is making me feel good about accepting this case or letting J be a part of it."

"Not much choice now. Unless you want to go back on your word. Plus, whatever this ghost has done, it won't just go away. We've got to deal with it."

"Any suggestions on that front?"

Sandra placed her hand on top of the open page. "Drummond, do what you can to talk with that ghost. Anything he can tell us will help. And if you can see the tether again, try to note any details — what color it is, how thick it is, anything at all. I'm going to research what I can here."

Max popped to his feet and gave his laptop a little shake. "I was heading off to my own research anyway. Guess I'll double my efforts."

With the team splitting off on their assignments, Max headed toward his new office tucked away in the back corner of the kitchen. Armed with a date of death and the name of a hometown, he figured he had a decent chance of finding out the name of their ghost soldier. He sidled into his little desk built into the tiny alcove and got started. Tried to, anyway.

His mind rehashed his earlier conversation with Sandra as well as J's behavior when presenting the case. His son had looked so excited, so thrilled to be dipping his toes into Max's world. What would he think when he learned that this ghost might not be so easy to get rid of?

Maybe Sandra was right. She usually was. But it seemed like the boys had only come under their guardianship a short while ago. How could so many years have passed already? How could it be possible that these boys were both teenagers? Heck, the simple idea that J had a date in two days befuddled Max. Now he had to deal with a ghost causing trouble.

Before he could fire up his laptop, the kitchen door to the outside opened and PB entered. A car backed out of the driveway, its lights flashing across the kitchen window. PB glanced over, gave Max a nod, and headed toward his bedroom.

Max said, "It's okay. I haven't started working yet."

PB paused, and Max swore he caught an irritated sigh before the boy turned back. "Hi, Max."

"Have a good day at school?" As with J, Max took a moment to notice how PB had changed. Broad shouldered now, the slim beginnings of a mustache, and the telltale crack in his voice. These changes had been brewing for a while now, but Max felt as if he saw them for the first time.

"School is fine, but I've got a lot of homework tonight, and it looks like you've got work to do, too. I'm really tired, and I don't want to be up all night, so if you don't mind —"

"Of course. Go do your work. Good night."

PB clumped off to his room, and as Max listened to the murmured conversations between the Sandwich Boys, he thought again about all that had transpired that day. Sometimes he wanted to hold the world still. But that only made it spin harder.

Opening his laptop, he shut out the uneasy sensations wriggling under his skin. Research — that's what he needed to do. The best cure-all for his worried mind.

The town of Whitten (or Widdin) did not appear in North Carolina on any map search. No surprise there. The ghost had a clouded mind and difficulty speaking. So, Max focused on the famous text *A Roster of North Carolina Troops in the War Between the States* by John Wheeler Moore. Published in 1881, the four volumes of Moore's *Roster* included the names of 106,498 soldiers from North Carolina, listing military units, service records, ranks, and remarks about everything from promotions to court marshals, injuries to captures, desertions to deaths. By cross-referencing the *Roster* with more modern Civil War registries and then comparing his findings to any man surviving the War in North Carolina with towns that began with the letter *W* or ended with *TEN* or *DIN*. Max eventually produced a list of nearly ten thousand names which could be their ghost.

As he organized and sifted through the endless information, Drummond drifted into the room. "Got our friend all squared away," he said.

Max lifted his head. "Oh? What'd you do with him?"

"I tried to show him the Other, but he wouldn't come. Probably can't since he's disconnected from his body. Not like me — he's disconnected in an unhealthy way. Clearly because of the tether and all. But I got him to understand he needed to give you some space to work. At least, I think he understands. He's pretty much hanging out across the street."

"It would really help if he could tell us his name."

"I tried to get that out of him. I did manage to get the first letter. At least, I think so. It's *A,* by the way."

"That will actually help a lot. If my data search on that comes up empty, we'll assume whatever he said was wrong and go from there."

Max returned to his laptop, adding the new parameters into his search — knocking down the list to three thousand names. After a few moments, he could feel the ghostly cold in the air. Looking up, he found Drummond staring back, arms crossed over his long coat.

"What?" Max said. "You got something else?"

Drummond tipped back his head. "When I was young — I mean little, like a kid — I had this friend, Paul Ricker. Everybody called him Pokey. His dad wasn't around much, always on the road — salesman of some kind. I was too young to care, so I never found out. But his mom — she was always around. Whenever we got together to play ball or shoot marbles or anything, she was there to see him off with a whole bunch of questions and concerns. She made sure he had a little bag with food even if we were only to be gone for thirty minutes.

"Back then, kids would get together in a little gang and go off into the woods or play on a baseball field or get in fights in the mud. Anything we wanted to do. As long as we were back for dinner. But not Pokey's mom. She treated him like he was made out of glass. Could break anytime."

"When I was a kid," Max said, "we called them helicopter parents — because they were always whirling around."

"We just called her a pain in the ass. Not to her face, of course. Anyway, things never changed for Pokey. Dad never was around and Mom was always around. By the time we became young men, when he got free of them, he went wild. Really crazy behavior. Far more than just drinking, too. He'd get hammered, pick fights, go whoring, drove like he had a death wish.

"I had been a beat cop for only a few months when I had to help a bunch of other cops break up a big street brawl. Guess who I ended up arresting?"

"I understand what you're trying to say, but I'm not being overprotective. I'm not worried about the boys getting a splinter or even breaking a leg from climbing in a tree. This ghost —"

"Is just another ghost. PB and J are teens now. Let them be that way while it's safe. Because if they have to wait until they're adults to act like stupid teens, that's when they'll end up in jail. If you're lucky."

Max poked the laptop keyboard with extra verve. "That's my point. It's not safe. This soldier is not *just another ghost.* Not all ghosts are nice like you. And I know you'll agree with me that we can't name a single witch who is trustworthy or safe."

"Sandra."

"Fine. But you can't name one who isn't my wife. I know there's no protecting the boys from the things we do entirely, look what's already happening to J, but there's no reason we have to dig them deeper into this hole."

"All I'm trying to say to you —"

"I heard you. But none of it'll matter if we can't find out who this ghost is and what threat he really poses to J. So, let me do my research. I'm sure Sandra is still working hard, too. Go in and tell her whatever you noticed about the tether."

After a few more keyboard taps, Max felt Drummond drift off. The house creaked as wind picked up outside. Nobody spoke within. Max and Sandra researched while the Sandwich Boys did their schoolwork.

The deeper Max delved into his search, the less he noticed the house, the boys, the creaking. It all drifted away like Drummond, like any ghost. And each time Max felt his body tire, he pushed harder. There would be no stopping that night, not until he found the answers they needed. Because no matter what Sandra learned, Max felt exactly as he did while sitting in Wake Forest Baptist Hospital. He knew the results already. Whatever this tether was, it spelled something awful for J.

Chapter 4

THE MORNING OPENED ON A GRAY DAY, one which promised plenty of drizzle and possibly a rainstorm or two. PB hurried through his morning routine, and when a car pulled into the driveway and honked the horn, the young boy dashed out of the house with goodbyes yelled over the shoulder. Max sat at the kitchen table watching this display of teenage energy and marveled that PB had become far more social than ever expected. He wanted to rush out, grab PB, and warn his son — teenagers could be horrible people and he needed to learn how to judge character. But Max thought about Drummond's helicopter parent story and he remembered that the only way one learned to judge character was by being burned a few times.

As he debated any action, Sandra entered the kitchen and motioned to the table. "I was thinking we should put this in the living room for the meeting."

"What's wrong with the kitchen?"

"Since our last office burned down, things haven't felt very official lately. The more official, the more professional. We'll inspire more confidence if we at least make an effort."

With an exaggerated groan, Max helped clear off the table. "You sure this is just about confidence? Perhaps you want to make things feel a little more special for a certain young man?"

As they maneuvered the table into the middle of the living room, Sandra grinned. "Nothing wrong with giving him some consideration. I think he deserves it. Besides, I called his school to tell them he was sick for the day. The poor boy might be on his last leg. Shouldn't we do everything we can to help him get better?"

Max chuckled. "I predict a miraculous recovery in the next

minute-and-a-half."

It took J closer to five minutes before he stumbled out of bed — completely healthy, of course. Another half hour went by with a shower and a quick bite. By the time they settled at the table, Drummond had already left his bookshelf and retrieved their ghost client — who, apparently, had not moved since being deposited across the street the day before. Max walked to the head of the table.

Whenever he made a presentation, he had the urge to move, to pace around. But with the sofa and chairs pushed aside and the kitchen table dominating the living room, he had little space to maneuver. Crossing his arms, he leaned back against the wall and waited until he had everybody's attention. Then: "Before I begin with what I've found, I'd like to welcome our adjunct member of the team — J."

Everyone applauded, causing J to blush. Sandra mouthed her thanks — she wanted something official, some consideration, so Max provided. He had to admit that J looked awfully pleased.

"Okay, on to work." Max gestured to the empty corner where he expected their client to be. "It took a while to find this guy's name, but once I had that, everything else fell in pretty quick."

J sat straight with a pen in hand and a legal pad on the table. He tried to appear serious — Max knew he was — but he could not hide the wide-eyed joy on his face. Glancing to the back corner, J said, "Don't hold back. What's his name?"

"Private Alexander Miller. Company C of the 45th North Carolina Regiment — the Guilford Light Infantry."

Drummond hovered near the dead private and gave a short nod. "Seems like that's right. Miller here has perked up."

"I'm going to go through everything I've learned, and since I'm the only one who can't see Private Miller, I trust you all to stop me if he indicates I've made a mistake. Ready?"

J jotted something on his legal pad. "Yup, I'm all ready."

Max suppressed his amusement — not hard to do when he saw Sandra and remembered that she would be making a presentation as well, one that could be a lot darker depending on what she found. "Okay, then. Here we go. Alexander Miller was born in 1845, in the town of Whitney, North Carolina. That part was more difficult to find than you'd think because Whitney barely exists anymore. We'll get to that in a little bit."

J scribbled furiously, and Sandra put her hand in his way. "You don't have to copy down everything he says. The pads are to make notes of what you want to bring up later and also for when we assign things to do."

"I know all that," J said. "But writing things down helps me remember."

"Then do what you need to do." She gestured for him to continue on. "You know best what you need."

Max said, "I don't have information on Miller's growing up or anything about his early life really. By the time I found the basics, I needed some sleep. But if we decide that information is pertinent, I should have little trouble digging something up. I do know that he spent most of his time during the Civil War here in North Carolina. Didn't see a lot of action which is probably why he remained a private, because I couldn't find any disparaging remarks about him. No court marshals, no reprimands, nothing to suggest that he had been a bad soldier. Yet for some reason, he ended up detached from the 45th in time to avoid Gettysburg and other major battles. Seems those in charge wanted him stationed near home. The fact that he also lived beyond the war furthers the point that he didn't see a lot of fighting."

"Why?" J said. "Lots of soldiers live through war."

"But this was the Civil War. During the big battles, a guy like Miller, one who did not stand out as a particularly good soldier — even if not a bad one — would certainly have been thrown to the front lines. I'm not saying he never was in a battle but not a lot of them. Not when he would've been considered cannon fodder."

Drummond said, "Miller's nodding. Not much for speaking, but he seems to understand enough of what you're saying to agree."

"Good. Then perhaps the other things I found out are also right."

"What about a rich or influential member of the family?

Maybe that's what kept him off the front lines. Wait — no. Miller's shaking his head at that."

"Doesn't really matter why he got out of the ugly side of the war. He did. After the war ended, Miller returned home to Whitney. From there, he lived a simple and quiet life. Got married years later, had five children — not uncommon amount for that time — and helped run the family general store. In 1902, he got sick with pneumonia, and that did him in. He was buried in the Whitney Cemetery, and the story should have ended there. But it's over a decade later that things got interesting."

While Sandra and Drummond showed a professional curiosity, Max had J riveted. He had to admit that it felt wonderful to have an audience again. Especially one that cared so greatly.

Stepping up to the table, Max set his hands on the wood and loomed over. "Several years after Miller died, the Alcoa company made a deal with the Governor. Alcoa started in 1888 and by this point, they had grown quite large. They produce aluminum and they wanted to start up a big factory in North Carolina. Like all governors, ours was hungry to bring in jobs, so he agreed to a large-scale plan in which they constructed a hydro-electric dam blocking up the Yadkin River to provide the extra power needed for the factory. It was completed in 1917, and then they flooded the land that covered several small towns, including the town of Whitney. This area became Badin Lake. Now, before they did the flooding, they had to relocate all the people in the towns as well as all the dead."

Drummond said, "I take it Private Miller didn't make the cut."

"There was no cut. Every last body was supposedly exhumed and relocated to one of the tallest hills in the area. Once flooded and the lake formed, that hill became an island. Conveniently called Graveyard Island."

J said, "So what's the problem?"

"Quite a few problems, actually. First, around three hundred bodies were moved and distributed amongst three graveyards on the island. But from the pictures I could find, these graveyards were not set up with any competent organization. They just dumped the bodies in holes and brought up the headstones. As far as we can tell, the correct headstones are on the correct bodies, so that's hopefully not an issue. But many of the headstones were damaged in the moving or just not maintained over the years. It's also difficult to get to the island. There's no road. You can follow a lone set of train tracks that cuts through which is several miles of walking from the leftovers of Whitney. Or you can hire a boat. Basically, though, we're looking at hiking. We probably can't afford the boat, and even if we could, we don't want to be drawing attention to the fact that we are nosing around that island."

"Sounds great," J said. "We hike out to Graveyard Island, find Miller's headstone, and match it up with his corpse. Right?"

"Is that all?" Drummond said. "Just find some random bones and match them with a grave that's eroded down to barely anything."

"He's not exactly wrong," Max said. "But as difficult as that would be, I think our problem is worse. I said before that all the bodies were supposedly exhumed. There's anecdotal evidence that not all made it onto Graveyard Island. The headstones made it, but the dam project was on a tight timetable, and I suspect the last round or two of corpses were simply left to be flooded. Based on how you all are describing the way Miller behaves and sounds, seems like part of him is stuck underwater. That's what I'm thinking happened to him, anyway."

Sandra stared at the soldier in the corner. "Miller appears to agree which means we're going to have to get his body from the bottom of the lake."

"Sorry, folks, but we can't do that," Drummond said. "I know a few things about Badin Lake. For one, it's uncommonly deep. You'd have to be an experienced diver to make it down to the bottom. And from the stories I remember in the 30s, that lake is a mucky, muddy mess. The chances of you being able to see anything down there is almost nothing. At least that's the way it was. Especially during World War II."

"What happened in World War II?"

"The Badin Bomber. Famous story — a couple bomber pilots were ferrying a new B-25 from Ohio to a Marine base near the North Carolina coast. The one guy lived near Badin and wanted to visit his fiancé, so he landed at a nearby airport, and brought his copilot to his home. Mama prepared a big feast and they drank and had a good time. Decided to spend the night, get up early, and deliver the plane before anybody was the wiser. But come morning, they're flying over the lake to tip their wings as a goodbye, and they circle the lake twice fine, but on the third time around something went wrong. The engines started to sputter and then a loud bang. The plane went down. Badin Lake swallowed it whole. During my days stuck in the old office, I would occasionally hear snippets of stories about that place. Divers would go down to check out the plane wreckage but had a heck of a time finding it. Too dark and murky down there. In fact, when you started this whole thing with Miller, I thought you were wrong about the Confederate soldier part and were going to end up telling me it was one of these young pilots who died."

Max tapped his chin as he looked over his notes. "Sorry to say it, but it seems to me that we might not be able to help this ghost. We can't afford to hire divers and we don't have the training to do it ourselves. From what Drummond says, it sounds like even if we did, we won't be able to find our way around down there, let alone locate an unmarked grave. Even if we managed to do all of that and somehow dig up those bones and bring them to the surface, we're still going to have a nearly impossible time finding where Miller is supposed to be buried on Graveyard Island. But, as was pointed out last night, we all get a say."

"For the moment," Sandra said, "I'm not sure any of us gets a say."

The dread sloshing within Max rose up his throat. "I guess it's your turn to talk, then."

Sandra stood and gave J a firm look. She launched into an overview of the problem with the ghost being tethered to him, bringing J up to the point where she did her night's worth of research. Then, making sure she had Max and Drummond's full attention, she continued. "There's a whole array of methods in which a ghost can become attached to a living being — that includes animals and fish and birds, too. Most of what we've dealt with in the past concerned ghosts tethered to an object or location, usually because of a curse, but it's not that different with a person."

"Somebody cursed me?" J said.

"Not exactly. The best I can tell is that one of two things has happened. Either somebody cursed Private Miller — perhaps forcing him to latch onto anybody who can see him — or, Miller has figured out how to tether on his own. He may have willfully, intentionally, attached to J in an effort to force us into helping him."

Drummond scratched his jaw. "Either way, why now? Miller's been dead since 1902. Plenty of viable candidates to attach since then, I imagine."

"I'm guessing he has attached to others before. When he's done with them, he's moved on."

"I don't like the sound of that."

Max swallowed hard. "None of this sounds good."

"It's not," Sandra went on. "If it's a curse, then it might harm J as collateral damage. But if it's intentional, and frankly, that's what I think we're dealing with, then Miller is slowly draining off part of J's energy."

J said, "Like my life?"

"Not quite that dark. The tether won't kill you. Not directly. Think of it like a feeding tube. You're sharing your life energy with Miller to keep him going. Now, you're a young, strong man, so you have plenty to share. Years and years' worth. But if Miller remains attached to you, then things get grim. You might end up weaker as you get older, susceptible to disease, and in the end, you'll die early in life because of this."

"Don't worry," Max said. "We won't let that happen."

"That's right, kid," Drummond said. "If I know your folks well, and I do, they'll figure out how to fix this. Right, Sandra? What's the plan?"

She paused as if weighing her options. But Max saw the

strength in her posture and knew she already had the decision made. Probably before she ever spoke.

"I'm going to cast a spell. Right now. You'll all help me. Breaking a tether like this is not something I've ever done, but we have to try. Miller died in 1902, but his ghost looks like the boy he was during the Civil War. If he was cursed, it probably happened then. But if he's the one targeting people, then he could be keeping his ghost-form young as a by-product of leeching their energy."

"Okay, doll, we don't need convincing. What do we do?"

"J — clear off this table. Max — I have everything sitting on our bed. Please bring it all here. Drummond — I need you to deal with Miller. Once we get started, he's not going to like this. And Mr. Miller — I promise you that whatever your curse, whatever you need to find rest, we'll help. But don't threaten this young man's longevity."

In moments, these tasks were completed. Sandra had taken the head of the table and gestured for Max and J to sit on either side. Drummond floated opposite her and kept a vigilant eye on Miller. In the center of the table, Max had placed a large green candle with a deep well at the top and a long wick.

Clasping Max and J by the hands, Sandra said, "I have been involved in several sophisticated castings, and I can perform all the basic spells on my own. To perform a spell of this difficulty alone is a bit new to me. Please, both of you, do what I ask, concentrate on what we're doing, and focus all of your love and support, all of your energy into my success."

Though she gripped his hand tight, Max could still feel the quiver in her fingers.

Chapter 5

FOLLOWING SANDRA'S INSTRUCTIONS, Max lit the green candle and cut off the lights. The morning sun had fully risen, but the overcast sky left the room dim and gray. The candleflame cut through the gloom creating a cozy warmth around the table. Or perhaps that was a result of Sandra's work.

"The green candle," she said, and J straightened. Max wanted to assure him that Sandra would take care of everything, but he stayed quiet. She had asked that they focus on her success and that's what he would do. He looked upon her and listened. She continued, "It symbolizes Mother Earth, the vessel of life that we all rely upon. It is Spring and growth and rebirth. A ghost is a remnant of Death, and its tether is a drain upon the living. Together, we will combat that leech, and like the leaves on the trees after winter, we will bring life back to where it had been taken."

From the bedroom, Max had brought more than just the large candle. Sandra picked up the second item — a bag of salt. She stood and drew a circle on the floor that encompassed the entire table. She tried to move with slow grace, but the table took up most of the space causing her to bump Max as she scooted by.

When she returned to her chair, she looked at Drummond. "Is Miller still in the corner? Outside of the circle?"

"You can see for yourself. He's right over —"

J started to turn in his chair but Sandra smacked the table. "No," she said. "For the remainder of this casting, the living must not look upon the tethered dead which we wish to cut loose. Understand?"

J's wide-eyed nod focused on his lap. "Yes, ma'am."

Max wanted to assure his son that everything would be fine,

but interrupting Sandra further would only undercut matters.

Sandra said, "Drummond, is Miller still in the corner?"

"Yeah. He's not looking too happy about all of this, but he's not looking like he's going to put up a fight, either. If he does, I'll stop him."

Sandra picked up a piece of green chalk. In front of each person, she drew a symbol onto the table. Max had seen Sandra cast many spells but never upon a table. Usually, she drew the spell out on the floor along the edges of the casting circle. By forming the circle around them, she had turned the table into part of the spell — at least, that was how he interpreted what he witnessed.

His chest swelled. Her ingenious method of bringing them into the casting circle — and, he noted, of keeping Miller out — raised Max's confidence toward their success. Sandra's impressive growth as a witch was on full display, and Max's pride in her grew alongside.

She slid a tattered book in front of her. The last item she had Max bring in from the bedroom, it traced back to the eighteenth century and had been one of Sandra's first acquisitions to begin her witch's library. She opened the book. The old cover crinkled like dry skin, and Max shuddered. Too many witch books had been made with real skin. He hoped that wasn't the case this time.

"Drummond?" she said.

"Still good. He's looking more curious, though. Maybe more concerned."

Putting out her hands, palms up, she looked from Max to J. "We join hands again to create a circle within the circle. A bond of family, love, and life."

Max held her hand once more and reached across the table to hold J's as well. He could feel energy pulsing between them — even if just their heartbeats — and it strengthened his sense of success. They were the Porter Agency, after all. Defeating the supernatural was their brand.

Sandra lowered her head over the book and mumbled words in an ancient tongue. Max had seen her do this so many times that it did not register in his mind — until J squinted in Sandra's direction. Squeezing the boy's hand, Max offered silent assurance that this part was normal.

For several minutes, nothing more happened. J fidgeted but Max made sure the circle remained closed. As if the furniture had also become impatient, the table bounced once. Not high, not hard, but enough to startle everyone.

After looking at both men, Sandra returned to her casting. Max, however, found it difficult to focus. The symbols she had drawn on the table glowed around the edges. Harsh green light shined up their faces like a campfire flashlight used to tell a scary story.

"Is this part normal, too?" J whispered.

"Shh," Sandra said. "Focus on my words. Focus on the power we are creating. Think of that bond between you and Miller — that line which connects. The tether."

J closed his eyes and lifted his head back. Max peeked at Drummond. The old ghost kept his eye on Miller like a dog staring at a field, knowing that something dangerous rustled in there and might come out at any moment.

As Max remembered he shouldn't look at the dead, the table hopped again. Then once more. It rattled from leg to leg, bumping Max's elbows as if it wanted to dislodge his hands, break the physical circle.

Drummond rose in the air, and Max's eyes darted toward the back corner. Though he couldn't see Miller, he did see a green filament of light stretching from that corner, across the room, and into J. Max had never thought of a ghost's tether as a real object, yet here he saw it. Perhaps only a manifestation caused by the spell, but it did exist.

"Max, pay attention," Sandra said. Then: "By the power of earth, the strength of rock, the force of wind." The table lifted a few inches into the air. "By destruction of flood and rebirth of fire, we dissolve that which should never have been."

Max's skin tingled — little pinpricks of electricity — and the hair on his body straightened. His mouth went dry. That green filament rose where it crossed the salt circle as if invisible fingers plucked it towards the ceiling.

Still clenching hands, Sandra lifted her arms above her head. "The living are the living, and the dead are the dead. Return both to where they belong. We break this binding, we shatter the curse of its existence, we cut ties that link those within this circle from those without."

She brought her arms down fast against the table as if chopping with a butcher's knife. The table smacked the floor, and bright green light flashed across the room. The air crackled like the start of a massive thunderstorm. But it never released. Just the loud crackle and then nothing.

Sandra lifted her arms a second time, and with her, the table rose. "We smash this link, destroy this connection."

Down came her arms, down came the table — and this time, the thunder arrived. The floor shook while a stampede rumbled from wall to wall. The instant the table hit the planking below, the wood in the center burst upward as if a fist had punched through from beneath. The green candle rolled off to its side, dribbling wax in its wake.

Sweating, Sandra collapsed back in her chair. They all turned their eyes to the green filament. Still there.

"Damnit," she said.

"Drummond?" Max said.

"Sorry, partner. Miller's still here, still tethered to J."

As J slumped, Sandra said, "I'm so sorry. Either I'm not skilled enough or whatever Miller did is stronger than I know how to deal with."

After a short silence, J said, "Isn't that the whole point of witchcraft? Using spells and such to pull off the impossible."

She cleared her throat as she looked from Max to J. "It's not impossible. It's just something I'm not experienced enough to do."

"Then I think we all know what needs to be done."

Max, Sandra, and Drummond exchanged looks, but as far as Max could tell, nobody had any clue what J meant. "And that is?" he finally asked.

"If we can't break the tether between me and Miller, then we have to go back to the initial case, right? We have to get his bones and bury them with his headstone on Graveyard Island."

Sandra said, "That might be more than we can handle. I mean, there are spells that move an object from one location to another. With some work, maybe I could come up with a variation that would be able to bring Miller's bones to the surface. But first you have to know where the object you want to move actually is. We don't know where the bones are — not specifically. And if we did, I'm still not sure I could make the spell work. Especially after this failure, I think that's a bit beyond my abilities."

"We can't do nothing," Max said.

"Of course not. We'll think of something."

"Wait, wait," J said. "Sandra, you said it's not impossible for everybody, just that you can't make it work."

Drummond shook a finger at J. "No, you don't want to think down that direction."

"Why not? You guys know lots of witches. Why don't we go find one that can pull off these spells? You've got to know somebody with enough experience."

Drummond floated over the table and looked down at J. "Kid, one of the first big lessons you need to learn in this business — and pay close attention here — you don't want to be relying on a witch. Ever."

"I couldn't agree more." Max sat. "The problem with all witches — other than Sandra — is that they don't ever work out of the kindness of their hearts. They expect to get paid. And it's almost never in cash. They'll want to make a special deal with you, and you should never go dealing with a witch."

"Unless," Sandra said, her attention off in her thoughts. "It's just that, thinking about this spell made me realize that all the witches we've known who are strong enough to succeed — well, they're all gone. Either they're dead or they ran away. All except one."

Max's throat tightened along with his chest. "No. We've done a good job of keeping our distance from her. Why should we go messing that up?"

"Because this is for J. Because sooner or later our paths will cross with her. If things go well, we can start off our relationship with North Carolina's head witch on a better footing than we have in the past with the former heads."

"She ain't wrong about that," Drummond said.

"Whose side are you on?" Max said.

"This time around, I'm on J's side. Fact is that we need some advantage over what's happening, some way to get Miller's bones to their resting place. We fail at that, J's looking at a slow and destructive future."

"Besides," Sandra said, "the worst thing that will happen is we talk it over with her and decide against whatever she's asking in payment. Then we're simply back to right now. But at least J knows we tried everything. At least, we'll know it, too."

Max knew better than to argue further. No point. Whether on purpose or not, Sandra had phrased everything to hinge on loyalty to J. And she was right. Drummond, too. They had to do all they could for J — even deal with a witch like Madame Ti.

"Fine. But I won't set this up through Cecily Hull. That's inviting too many problems."

"I wasn't going to ask you to, anyway. I think it best that I approach Madame Ti on my own terms. One witch to another."

"See if you can get her to buy us a new table, too."

Sandra nudged one of the legs which had split down the middle. "I think that might be pushing our luck with her."

Max agreed even as he shook his head. Madame Ti. Damn.

Chapter 6

NOT WANTING TO WASTE THE AFTERNOON, and not wanting to face J's growing apprehension, Max drove off to visit his mother. He needed to speak with her, anyway — assuming she would even answer the door — but he also needed to escape his apparently insane family. Madame Ti? Bad enough to trust any witch, but Madame Ti? At least Drummond had agreed that it was dangerous, even if the ghost supported the idea. But more than anything, what really convinced Max to go along with approaching Madame Ti was a point Sandra later made in private.

"I know you're scared about bringing that witch into this case," she had said.

"More than scared. We're talking about J. He's already been too close to some of the crazier parts of what we do. Now he's got to deal with a tethered ghost, too. Can't we wait a few years until he's an adult before springing him into dealing with witches? At least, he'll be more able to make a rational choice."

"That's the piece your missing, honey. We don't have a choice."

"Sure, we do. J is still a kid. Fine, fine, a young adult. Whatever you want call him, we can simply not allow him to be part of this yet."

"Ah, yes, we'll not allow him. Just tell this teenager he can't do something. That'll solve it."

"I know, but sitting back while he runs headfirst into madness is, well, madness."

She stroked his chin with a loving touch. "I wish it were as easy as not allowing him to do it. But this ghost, Alexander Miller, he could have attached himself to any witch, any medium, any psychic, any person with the gift of seeing ghosts, but he went after J. That's not an accident."

"You said it could also be a curse."

"I did. But I doubt that. J has some serious power within him, and it's attractive to those who can see it."

Max bent low and held her tight. "What are you saying?"

"This won't be the last time. Others will be lured by what they see, what they feel in him. We've got to help J learn how to control what he has. Learn to use it and not succumb to it. Learn how to deal with those who would want to curse or exploit him for it. That starts now. With this case. With Madame Ti. Because if we don't help Miller get to rest, he might do more than simply follow J around, more than drain J over decades. He might haunt our son."

Max closed his eyes. "And that would push J to research spells to get rid of the ghost."

"Which would lead into deeper witchcraft — and not the kind we want him exploring."

Pulling Sandra close, feeling her breath against his neck, he said, "Promise me that we'll do all we can to keep J and Madame Ti as far apart as possible."

"Absolutely."

With nothing more to be done until Sandra went through her witch channels to set up the meeting, J was given the choice of going back to school for the second half of the day or staying home and doing research on the Civil War. No surprise, he chose the latter.

With his family settled in, Max had other business to handle that day. But by the time he sat on the long couch in his mother's apartment, he began to think J had the smarter idea. If Max had gone to a library, he could have buried his head in research about Alexander Miller. Or he could have gone to Lexington, parked at Speedy's or good ol' Lexington Barbecue, and sat in front of a big, hot plate of chopped pulled pork. At least, that was a pleasant way to devour one's troubles.

His mother shuffled in from the kitchen carrying a tray with two cups of coffee. She looked ten years older. Max had always heard that going to the hospital meant the beginning of the end for the elderly. Now, he wondered if the real culprit behind the idea wasn't that the germs would attack the aging immune system but rather what such visits did to the will. Perhaps his mother would have been better off never getting diagnosed. Especially since there was no cure. She could now put a name to the thing destroying her body but nothing more.

"How is PB getting along in his new school?" she asked with the calm of an easy summer afternoon as she set the tray on a glass coffee table.

Max reached for the cup but held back. He couldn't stomach the idea of pretending. Yet despite those thoughts, he said, "He's doing well. Surprisingly."

"Why *surprisingly?* You didn't think I would do a good job preparing him for the inevitable transition?"

"I didn't mean it like that. I only meant that high school can be a difficult environment, even when you've been in it for a long time. It's all new to PB."

"He's got his brother to help him."

"They're two years apart. In teenage years, that's like being a decade apart."

Mrs. Porter rolled her eyes as she sipped her coffee. "You're going to have to be smarter than that if you want to survive the teen years. I know. You were no picnic during that time, let me tell you."

"We'll do fine with it. You don't have to worry." He marveled at how relaxed she appeared, how simple the conversation bounced between them, yet part of him rebelled. Part of him insisted that he stop placating and get to the core of things. As much as he wanted to ignore that part within, his marriage had taught him the benefits of facing an uncomfortably reality head-on. No more stalling. He cleared his throat. "I wanted to talk to you about all that's happened because you don't need to worry about any of it. Sandra and I are here for you."

Setting her coffee cup down with a sharp clack, she said, "Don't you start that."

"Start what?"

"Don't you wrap me up in cushions and pillows and bubble wrap and start acting like I'm this fragile thing that will crack if I get bumped around. We're going to have to face enough real problems with multiple sclerosis. Yes, I can say the words. See? We don't need to manufacture more problems."

"That's not what I'm trying to say."

A wisp of gray hair stuck out above her ear. Max wanted to set it in place, but he thought the gesture might be misinterpreted.

"I don't know if you remember this, you were quite young when it happened, but a long time ago, I had to go visit a doctor. I couldn't bring you along. This was a woman's doctor, and while many patients brought their children, I've never thought that was appropriate. At least, back then. Times change. Probably wouldn't give it a second thought now. Anyway, I only had one good friend to watch you. Do you remember her? Minnie Borich? Well, you weren't having it. Threw a full tantrum."

"Stop it." He had not intended to sound so harsh. He had not intended to interrupt at all. But a rebellion of emotion surged up through his chest and heated his neck.

Mrs. Porter stared at Max as if she had been slapped. Even brought her hand to her cheek. Her questioning brow pushed him into silence. He wanted her to understand without having to voice anything. He needed her to understand. She had to see that this sudden dwelling in the past sounded like an acceptance of Fate — of Death. He had no room for such acceptance.

He scooted closer on the couch. Holding her hands, he whispered, "You can't give up."

And with those words spoken, with their sounds dying on the empty air, he crumpled to his knees. The sobs rolled up from his stomach and surged through his shoulders. His eyes stung as the tears poured out. Mrs. Porter rested her hands on his head, stroked his hair, and that simple kindness — that motherly kindness — wracked his body with wave after wave of deeper sorrow.

"It'll be okay," she said, soft and gentle.

"It's not right. Not fair."

She chuckled. "When has Life ever been right or fair?"

Trying to regain his composure, he sniffled hard before sitting back. "How can you be so calm?"

"Because, my sweet boy, I have you to take care of me, and I know you'll do a wonderful job." She leaned across the coffee table and snatched two tissues which she handed over. "Might take a little training, but you'll get the hang of it. You'll be great at it. Eventually."

After blowing his nose, he said, "You're the one taking care of me."

"And this is the last time. After today, no more. You aren't allowed to behave this way anymore. Our roles are about to reverse, and I'm going to have to rely on you. That's the natural way of things. The parent takes care of the child, and in the end, the child takes care of the parent. Can I rely on you?"

"Of course. You know I'll be here for you. Always."

Grabbing her coffee, Mrs. Porter crossed her legs and smirked. "Look at the bright side — after I'm dead, you won't have to listen to Sandra complain about me ever again."

Max stared at her, stunned, and then broke out into laughter.

That night, when he returned home, Max walked by the Sandwich Boys' room on his way to the bathroom and overheard PB saying, "No, man. Porn isn't real. You gotta treat a woman with decency. The rest of that stuff will happen, but if you spend the whole date trying to make moves into her pants, you'll probably fail and you'll miss out on the entire date."

Max had to pause. PB giving J dating advice — especially good advice — filled Max with a warmth that had been missing most of the day. Since PB had never been on a date, Max was even more impressed.

"— and when the movie's going on," PB said, "all you have to do is raise your arms in a big stretch, and then when you settle them down, you have your one arm around her shoulder."

"Then what?" J asked.

Max wanted to barge in the room and explain that then he

would be stuck with his arm around that girl's shoulder for the next two hours, that the circulation would die all the way to his fingertips, leaving his arm numb and useless. The better way would be to hold her hand, making sure to share the armrest so neither one had that hunk of barely-padded metal digging in. But Max stopped himself.

If he burst in there and started spouting off advice, they wouldn't listen. If anything, they might get angry at his eavesdropping. Or worse they might think he tried to control them — control their behavior. No, he had to come up with a smarter way to deal with the changes they were going through.

Besides, he could always talk with J in the morning.

Chapter 7

FRIDAY MORNING. Before Max ever had a chance to speak with J, the Sandwich Boys had sped off to school like squalls bursting through the kitchen, grabbing food, and exiting to storm other lands. Granted, he had been late getting out of bed, and an argument could be made that he had not tried hard to reach J before the boys left, but Max also knew he lacked the right words to say all the things on his mind. Yet. He needed time to think through matters. While he knew nothing about parenting a teenager, he felt fairly confident that any misspoken phrase would be trotted out at a later date to be used against him. Parenting needed its own Miranda warning. He had enough hauntings of the ghostly variety to deal with, he didn't need to be haunted by his own words for the rest of his life.

Besides, J's laughter had reverberated through the small house that morning, and Max did not want to damper the boy's happiness. J's first date would be that night. Clearly, he had decided that he wouldn't let being attached to a ghost stand in his way. Or perhaps his faith in the Porter Agency to fix matters left him hopeful and able to focus on his future. Max had to marvel at the resilience of youth.

His own future did not look as bright. Sandra had arranged a meeting with Madame Ti for one o'clock that afternoon. Max didn't really want to know how she had acquired the appointment, but she told him anyway. According to her, it had proven to be quite easy, in fact. Unlike previous head witches of North Carolina, Madame Ti welcomed listening to the concerns, ideas, and grievances of all the witches and covens around. At least, she made a show of listening.

"Whether she'll actually pay attention to any of it is another matter," Sandra had said. "And don't let that open-door policy fool you — though she's not brash in the way she controls the witches of North Carolina, Madame Ti has proven to be shrewd and quietly vicious."

"Speak softly and carry a big stick type?"

"Yeah. Except you can do a lot more damage with witchcraft than a big stick."

With several hours to go before partaking in this meeting he did not want to partake in, Max thought his time would be better spent by working than fretting. If they managed to convince Madame Ti into raising Miller's bones from the depths of Badin Lake, they still needed to know where to bury them. Mapping the headstones of Graveyard Island's three cemeteries would help more than anything else Max could think to do.

He began by visiting his usual graveyard websites and lamented the fact that he led a life which included the phrase *usual graveyard websites.* These sites listed every person buried throughout the state, providing burial dates, locations, and epitaphs given. Unfortunately, Graveyard Island had not been catalogued by anybody. Normally, if a cemetery was owned by a church, then the church uploaded burial information to the database. Same with synagogues and mosques and anybody in charge of keeping track of the dead.

But Graveyard Island did not appear to have any specific owner. Probably Alcoa or the state claimed the land, but the graves were simply an afterthought. After some deeper searching, however, Max managed to find several hiker reports. These came in many forms, but the idea ran similar throughout them all — a hiker or group of hikers left online reports of the trails they blazed throughout the world and the unique features they discovered. Oftentimes, these hikers would come across graves — part of forgotten family plots, unmarked burials, or in the case of Graveyard Island, the three cemeteries.

In several cases, these hikers took the time to catalog the names and other information they could read off the eroding headstones. The better hikers provided coordinates for each grave — quite useful considering the lack of any logical arrangement given to these particular graves. Most graveyards either buried the dead in straight rows and columns or in conformity with the contours of the land. But on Graveyard Island, the bodies appeared to be scattered about as if somebody had strewn pebbles on a map and wherever they landed marked where a body would be buried.

Max also stumbled on a YouTube video some paranormal investigators had made. It depicted the long walk along the railroad tracks toward the island. A half-dozen young people trudged all the way out with lots of chatter and heavy breathing. When they finally reached the island, they got confused and disoriented. Not in a mystical way. They were simply exhausted and lacked a map. They never did see a ghost.

None of this gathered information directly placed Private Alexander Miller's grave to any singular spot, but it did narrow the options. At the very least, Max could mark locations on the map where Miller's grave could not be. Slow going, meticulous work, but Max dug into it with vigor.

When Drummond had floated in, ready for their visit with Madame Ti, Max never noticed. It took Drummond's strong voice calling for Sandra to join them before Max lifted his head. The old detective tipped his hat as Sandra entered. He had something to share.

"With everything you've already found out," Drummond said, swaying with his hands in his coat pockets, "I figured I could make use of my time by asking around the Other about Miller. Not as many ghosts from the Civil War hang around the Other — most have either moved on or are too traumatized by that war to do anything but haunt the world — yet there are some. Nice fellows, too. Amazing how being removed from all the bile of the Confederacy and the self-righteousness of the Union left these young men with over a hundred years to grow up. The racism is gone. The savior complex is gone. The animosity is gone. All that's left are people who care about their families and each other. Frankly, if these guys could be reborn as modern politicians, they'd save the world."

"Pity it takes death and a century to drain all that hate out of people," Max said.

Sandra said, "I take it that these born-again Civil War veterans shared something about Miller that's useful."

Clicking his tongue, Drummond said, "That's the thing — nobody would talk about it."

Max stopped his grave marking. "I thought you had a whole network of snitches."

"None of them were willing to give me anything. Not even Miss 1800s, and she's still crazy for me."

Sandra said, "You think all of them could be afraid of Private Miller?"

"Doubt it. Not afraid of a witch, either. It's rare for a living witch to be able to hold influence in the Other — not impossible, of course. You've heard me talk about it happening before, but it's particularly rare. Fact is, in my nearly eighty years of death, I've only ever seen it happen that one time. And even then, the witch failed to strike fear in all of the ghosts."

"Well, that's great." Max slammed shut his laptop. "This was supposed to be a minor little case to help J get his feet wet. Then we learn that Miller's actually an attached ghost with lost bones and possibly a threat to J's longevity. And now, he's apparently a ghost that's freaking out all the ghosts in the Other. Can we all agree that this keeps taking steps into a much darker and more dangerous path?"

"No argument from me. But don't think that's going to change matters regarding J."

"Why not?"

"You want to handle this one, doll?"

Sandra moved closer to Max and by doing so, changed the timbre of the entire room. She was like the pink hues of dawn cracking over the dark horizon. "Think it through, honey. How will J see it? This is his first big case, one that he brought to us, and he's already shown that he can't be deterred off it with ease."

"We're the parents here. We put our foot down. It's too dangerous."

"We can do that. But not without consequences."

"He'll be mad, that's all. He'll get over it. We'll try again after we dislodge Miller and find a safer case."

"You're focusing on the wrong thing. If we throw him off this case, if we really do that, then we'll destroy any trust he has in us."

"What, then? We're just expected to let him walk into something so frightening that even the ghosts in the Other don't want to talk about it?"

Sandra gave Max a long hug. "What we do is treat him like a full member of the team. He'll face the same threats that we all do. Because anything else is doomed to fail, will ruin our relationship with him, and in the end, he'll simply be that much less prepared to deal with future cases. Not to mention whatever the results from Miller turn out to be."

Max pictured that first day from long ago — PB and J sitting in his downtown office. The way J looked when PB first suggested that if he was going to work for Max, then J had to be hired, too. Tough, defiant, streetwise and doubting all the possibilities of the world. "He's so young."

"Not as young as you think. We'll use everything in our power to make sure he comes through this in one piece. Just like we do for each other." She kissed Max's cheek and stepped back. "That starts with the three of us going to meet Madame Ti. You see? I'm sure J would love to join us today, but no matter how much he might think it's cool to talk with a witch like her, we have to make sure that never happens."

"Finally, something I agree with. I think I even made that point recently."

"That's how we'll protect him. It's the only way."

Drummond clapped his hands together once. "Okay. Good. That's settled. Let's hop to it and get this over with."

Chapter 8

AT NOON, THE DRIZZLE BEGAN, and by one o'clock, rain drove down in sheets. Max and Sandra stood under the canvas awning of a funeral parlor in the city and listened to the drumbeat. Drummond had the decency to float in the rain so as not to crowd the two living people with his ghostly chill, but Max shivered anyway.

"Should we knock on the door?" he asked.

Sandra glanced at the entrance with a raised eyebrow. "We're not going in there. We're waiting to be picked up."

The wind blew harder, sending sharp-bullet raindrops against their bodies. Max put his back into the gusts while Sandra bounced from one foot to the other in front of him. Trying to keep warm, they huddled closer. At length, a gray minivan pulled alongside the curb. The side door slid open, and the driver waved them in.

Max and Sandra scooched across the bench seat as the side door closed. A ruby-haired woman turned back and smiled. "Hi there," she said with a strong North Carolinian accent. "My name's Ruby." She rolled her eyes to look at her hair.

"Nice to meet you. I'm Max and this is Sandra."

"And your ghost is Drummond, right?"

Drummond had settled into the passenger seat, but Ruby did not look at him. Interesting. "That's right," Max said. "Where are we headed?"

"Sorry. Y'all don't get to know that."

She pulled into traffic with her windshield wipers slapping back and forth rapidly. They weaved their way down to 1st Street and out of the city, passing the baseball stadium, and curving south onto Peters Creek Parkway.

"Will this drive take long?" Max asked.

Ruby peeked in the rearview mirror. "Time is a relative construct. Would you like some music?"

"No, thank you."

She flicked on the radio and tuned to a classic rock station.

"Oh, she's a real peach." Drummond said, and Max could picture the spit flying off his mouth — if a ghost could do such a thing.

They continued south for nearly twenty minutes. The rain backed off and finally stopped, but the water spluttering off the road dotted the windshield. As the sun broke through cracks in the clouds, they pulled off at an abandoned gas station. A maroon minivan had been parked along the side near the restroom doors. Ruby stopped next to it.

"Transfer time."

Max and Sandra crossed over into the other minivan as Drummond floated through with them. After sitting in the driver's seat, Ruby handed back two black blindfolds.

"Really?" Sandra said. "We have a ghost with us. He's going to be able to tell us exactly where we are."

"I don't make the rules." Ruby started the engine and waited.

With a huff, Max said, "Okay. But I warn you, I might fall asleep wearing one of these things."

As Sandra tied on her blindfold, she added, "Drummond, you know what to do."

"Don't worry," the old ghost said. "I'll make sure you know exactly where we end up."

Even without Drummond's help, Max felt confident he knew the direction they drove in. North. In fact, Ruby made little effort to disguise that they retraced the same path they had come down. No winding turns, no blasting music to hide sounds, nothing to prevent Max from listening and feeling and keeping track of their path. But he did have Drummond which not only confirmed his suspicions but added a few items Max could not tell — or, at least, he would not have been able to tell until the blindfolds were removed.

"Will you look at that," Drummond said, and Max had to bite

back a sarcastic comment pointing out that he couldn't look at anything. "Ruby here is wearing a wig. Looks like she's more Blondie now."

As they drove on, Max felt Sandra's hand crawl over. Their fingers laced together. He could read in her grip that she wasn't nervous — just keeping their unity strong. He leaned closer and kissed her on the cheek.

"We're back in the city," Drummond said as the sound of rain pattered against the rooftop. "She's turning onto Broad Street."

Still heading north. Another turn on 5th Street, and then another on Summit. If Ruby thought she could confuse Max by doubling back and crossing to the other side of town, she didn't know anything about him — the streets of Winston-Salem were old friends.

Plus, he had a ghost watching everything. Which they had told her. That suggested that either she didn't believe them about Drummond or her orders required her to take this specific path, no matter how pointless.

After several more turns, however, the van took an unexpected right, dipped down a tight ramp, and came to a stop. Max tried to think of what parking structure went down in such a way at this location, and he came up empty.

"We're just off Motor Road," Drummond said. "Near that tractor company, but I can't say I knew about this parking structure. From the outside, it's nothing but some homes. Under here, though, it's kind of impressive."

Ruby said, "You can take a look now."

Max and Sandra removed their blindfolds. They were in a parking garage, but one set up for private use. Though large enough to house at least ten cars, Max saw only the minivan and one other — a red 911 Porsche, probably from the 1980s.

"This way," Ruby said, indeed wearing blonde hair now. Her accent had dropped away, too.

She led them to a service elevator capable of loading in one of the cars. With their footsteps echoing, they entered the elevator. Ruby never dropped her personable smile as they descended, but it looked forced and somewhat professional —

like a butler of a grand estate.

Max lost track of how long they went down — certainly longer than it would take to go one or two floors. When they stopped, Ruby pressed a few buttons to open the elevator. Humid, sour air assaulted them as if they had opened onto a trash heap.

She said, "My apologies about the stink. The sewer system is a little above us, and the smell gets everywhere. Follow me."

She led the way along a narrow path dug out of the rock. It reminded Max of taking a guided tour through Linville Caverns. There were even spotlights set up along the way to prevent people from tripping.

Above, he could hear the rush of water through the sewer tunnels. The rains must have increased the regular flow. As they moved, he saw Sandra scanning the area, but she never spoke. Even Drummond remained quiet and observant.

Max couldn't help but think of Madame Yan — another witch who had lived underground. But Madame Yan's abode had required a stooped over hike across a wide crawlspace. And her actual dwelling looked like all witch homes — a hoard of collected trinkets covering floor to ceiling. Newspapers, shoes, stuffed birds, old food containers, teeth, and boxes upon boxes of oddities Max hardly wanted to remember. All that before she emptied the hidden home and skipped town.

The size of Madame Ti's underground abode, however, made Madame Yan look like a pauper. He feared they might die under the weight of the junk Madame Ti would have filled this cavern with.

When they reached a metal door — rusting and wet with the humidity — Ruby gestured to a wooden bench in front of some cubby holes. "Shoes," she said. "Please."

Max fought hard to keep his mouth shut as he sat on the bench and removed his shoes. After setting them in a cubby, he gestured for Ruby to hurry up and continue.

"Perhaps you would prefer to wait until your wife is ready?" She raised her index finger to silence any retort. Once Sandra cubbied her shoes, Ruby knocked twice on the door. "You may enter. I'll be waiting right here to take you back when you're done."

Max wanted to turn back right then. Or at least ask a dozen questions. Or maybe level a few choice words to their chauffer. But Sandra never gave him the chance. She opened the door and entered.

Chapter 9

THE ROOM WAS DARK. And wide. Wide enough that in the center, four white candles mounted on long gold poles could not reveal the walls. If that didn't prove it, Max heard little echoes of sound bouncing around to hit him with the size of the place.

He stepped forward and his socked feet fell upon a thick Turkish rug. As he moved ahead, one rug after another met his path. They spread out in all directions creating a mosaic of carefully crafted geometric shapes and dark colors. The candles formed a large square and in the center of this lit area — at least, Max thought of it as the center — a poised, worldly woman wearing red silk perched upon a small hill of pillows.

"Not very witch-like," Max said to Sandra.

"Don't let it fool you. She's the most dangerous witch around."

As they approached, Madame Ti gestured to two pillows opposite her. "Good afternoon. I apologize for my accommodations. Taking control of magic in an entire state is not an easy task, and whenever you take control of power that others thought they held, it creates enemies. I have to be a bit extra cautious for the time being. I'm sure you understand."

As Max settled on a soft pillow, he said, "Of course." Well, he understood the *enemies* part, at least.

Drummond hovered at a respectful distance. "Just want to point out to you both that I'm here. Haven't encountered a single ward or spell of deflection or anything else that would stop a ghost. In other words, she's either cocky as all get out or she's so powerful, there isn't a need for her to worry about basic protections from the paranormal."

Max tried not to show the growing unease in his stomach.

"Thank you for seeing us. Our situation is —"

"No, no." Madame Ti raised one finger. "First, hospitality."

Without any signal that Max could catch, Ruby rolled out a cart filled with tea, coffee, and cookies. Her hair had changed again — this time brunette — and she had given up her personal smile for a stern look of concentration. As she gestured toward the cart, she showed no sign of recognizing Max or Sandra.

Twins? Max wondered.

"No, thank you," he said. Ruby made the offer to Sandra who also politely declined. Once more, without a signal from their host, Ruby pushed the cart off into the unseen ends of the room.

Madame Ti opened a small clutch and pulled out a cigarette. She offered the open pack to Max and Sandra but they shook their heads. "You have come to my home, you have turned away my offer of refreshment, and now you turn away a cigarette. You're being quite rude."

"No offense was intended," Sandra said. "We simply don't smoke."

Max gestured to the room. "Plus, we've had a few years of experience dealing with witches. Nothing is ever offered for free — even tea and cookies."

Madame Ti puffed smoke into Max's direction. "Things change, Mr. Porter. Tricking fools into lopsided deals has done nothing but perpetuate the bad stigma we witches hold in the world. That was the way of our ancestors, and to some degree, they had to play those games in order to survive. It doesn't have to be that way anymore."

"You're going to change things?"

"I did not go through all my hardships to earn this position simply for my own gain and to lord over the witches like my predecessors."

"Funny, you seem to be lording over them quite well. They're scared of you."

"As they should be. But that doesn't mean I'm going to keep every witch on a leash. Rather, I hope to allow them plenty of freedom to explore new avenues of witchcraft and create new spells. I want them to be witches in the fullest sense. But, of course, we must acknowledge and deal with the reality of the world we live in. While it's true that many witches can be out in the open now — many institutions even recognize the Wiccan religion — it's also true that the majority of people remain ignorant of who and what we really are. They fear us. They fear what they don't understand. They fear because of the lies they've been taught. Centuries of lies."

"Lies?"

"People trust the sources of information that tell them what they want to believe. Even when those sources are blatant liars. The lies become the trusted truth and everything else becomes the lie. And when you get people believing in such a thing year after year, when they ingest it to the point that they can no longer accept reality, they can get dangerous. Why do you think so many witches were burned at the stake? Propaganda. Lies."

"I don't know. Most of the witches we've encountered have been quite dangerous."

"Most of the witches you've encountered do not reflect most of the witches in the world. The majority of our women have no interest in controlling people or warping the fortunes of the future."

"That's because most who call themselves witches cannot access the seriously alarming magic that you all can."

"I suppose if we limit the word *witch* to only reflect those of us who wield true power, then the conversation sounds quite different."

Drummond snorted a chuckle. "I don't care what you call her. Don't forget what she really is."

Madame Ti eyed the direction Drummond floated in before continuing. "Of course, if the non-witches would stop bothering us, stop coming to us for spells that they don't understand how to use, I suspect history would be very different. Did you know that the practice of making deals started as a way of limiting non-witches from bothering us? It's true. We thought that if the price was set high enough, they'd leave us alone to commune with nature. The non-witches would be left to do what they do. Mostly destroy themselves." She took a long drag on her cigarette. "I find it amusing that you have such a low opinion of witches. You're married to one, after all."

"Sandra's a very different kind of witch. A new kind. One that's not interested in power or mind games."

"Is that right?"

Sandra said, "There's a lot of good that can come from witchcraft, but so much of what we do has been perverted by the less than moral."

"In the propaganda."

Sandra nodded. "I'll give you that."

"Why thank you. I'm so relieved to know that Sandra Porter allows me my opinion." She stabbed the cigarette out in a glass bowl. "You say you want to be a different kind of witch? Well, I want to create a different kind of witch community. And unlike you, I have positioned myself with the power to do so. It's not mind games, it's — well, I suppose it's a form of politics. As disgusting as that may be. And like any good politician, I'm here to listen to what you want. Now, tell me."

Max looked to Sandra thinking that, as a witch, she might be better suited to telling their story. She looked back with a nudge of her head suggesting that as the one who does all the research and traditionally shares all the information, he might be the better choice. Max inclined his head to the side emphasizing that one witch to another made more sense. Sandra raised her eyebrows as if considering the idea but then gave a little shake indicating that he would watch his words with this witch to a greater extent. Max frowned and—

Madame Ti glared at them both. "I am responsible for all the witches of North Carolina, and that takes significant time. Please stop wasting mine."

With a shrug, Max said, "It's like this." And he launched into the full details of Private Alexander Miller. He gave every bit of knowledge he had about Miller's life, death, burial, exhumation, and reburial, or lack thereof. He left out only one item — J. As far as he was concerned, Madame Ti never needed to know J had any part in this case.

Max concluded, "We need a witch powerful enough to locate

Miller's bones from the bottom of Badin Lake and transport them to us on the island. We know there are several witches who can accomplish this, but we wanted to respect your leadership as well as your own strength as a witch."

Madame Ti raised the corner of her mouth. "Then I agree."

Max looked to Sandra. Stuttering, he said, "Y-You do? Just like that?"

Madame Ti chuckled. "Of course not. There's always a cost to a witch's work."

"But what about all that talk of change?" Sandra asked.

"Doesn't happen overnight. If I don't exact a cost, the other witches will think I'm weak. If they see weakness, they'll strike. I can't very well alter the course of the witch community if I lack the position to do so."

"Here it comes," Drummond said. He drifted a bit closer. "I'm only going to say this once because you both should know better by this point — you can't trust this woman."

Max had no argument to that. The three of them knew the dangers of dealing with a witch. It was an occupational hazard. One which Max readily avoided. But this time, avoiding this deal meant ending the case, meant failing J, and possibly setting J up to attempt something stupid on his own. That last point stuck with Max more than any other. J knew only enough to get himself in trouble — and with an attached ghost, trouble already surrounded him.

"What do you want?" Max asked, hoping not to sound defeated.

"Your soul will do."

"What?"

"Relax. Just a little witch humor. However, these spells you're asking of me, well, that's a tall order. Such difficult spells are not going to come cheaply." As Madame Ti thought, she dug out another cigarette from her clutch and lit up. "In fact, it occurs to me that were these spells easier, Sandra could handle them herself. You suggested there were others you thought to ask, but no — that's not true. Coming to me with this request means it's not only far beyond what you or others are capable of, but that it's far more time sensitive. After all, if the matter could wait for you to learn, I know you'd eventually be able to cast the spell. You've got great potential."

"And you talk a lot," Max said.

"Not usually. However, your wife is fascinating, and I also have fewer interactions of late. But that is my problem, not yours. For your problem, what I require is rather simple — a promise."

In a cold tone, Sandra said, "Not all promises are simple."

"This one is such that it may never come to be. In fact, if things go as I intend, I will never need you to fulfill this promise. But I do like insurance."

Trying not to sound impatient, Max gritted his teeth. "What's the promise?"

"All of my predecessors have had a delicate balance with the Hull family. They've been powerful spellcasters in their own right and so controlled the head witch as much as relied upon her. But Cecily Hull and I are attempting a different sort of balance. One based on the fact that, unlike her predecessors, Cecily Hull does not use magic. She requires me in all things witch related."

Max's stomach churned. "I think I see where this is going."

"There may be a time when Cecily Hull decides she no longer wants me around, when she decides to follow in her family's footsteps and learn witchcraft on her own. Should that happen, should I be required to go against her, well, I will need people on my side. No matter when this happens — tomorrow or twenty years from now — the witches will undoubtedly split down the middle. Many will stay loyal to me, and many will side with the Hulls. Having the Porters on my side will help tip the scales. But, as I say, none of that need ever happen. Your promise to side with me will most likely never be called."

Drummond clicked his tongue. "You ask me, she's already planning to rise against the Hulls and is shoring up her strength."

"I might add that the witch community has already become far more stable under my leadership than under any other head in the last hundred years. I only desire to continue bringing that stability to my constituents, as it were."

"Oh, sure. That's why you're meeting her under a sewer. Real bang-up job she's doing."

Max leaned over to Sandra. "Any promise that sounds this easy can't possibly be good."

Sandra said, "I know, but if we don't do this, if we don't give this our best effort, what about J? He'll never trust us."

Madame Ti said, "J will definitely find out."

Max and Sandra jumped to their feet. Pointing his finger at Madame Ti, his face burning with fury, Max said, "Don't you ever go near my sons. You understand? You think the Porters are so easily manipulated? You don't know our history with the witch world. You should ask around."

With an equally firm finger pointing, Madame Ti said, "I do my homework. I know all about your strengths and, more importantly, your weaknesses. Both of you best sit back down and discuss this with respect or you will suffer for it."

"That's it," Drummond said, soaring up to Madame Ti. "I've had it with this witch."

Madame Ti's head cocked towards Drummond. "And I've had it with you snooping around instead of making yourself clearly known." She flicked her hand as if brushing an insect out of the air. Drummond disappeared. "He'll be waiting in the garage for you."

Max said, "You shouldn't have done that. He hates it."

"I don't really care. Now, sit."

With her hand on her hip, Sandra said, "You do not get to command us around. We've made no deal."

Placing her hand on her chest like a debutante in shock, Madame Ti said, "Oh, my word — are you truly under the impression that there is still a negotiation to be had? My dear, that was over the second you entered this building. There is no more to discuss. You will agree to my cost."

"And if we don't?"

"Well, I obviously won't do the spells for you. However, you have taken up quite a bit of my time today. That time costs. You'll still have to pay me for that. I strongly suggest you simply accept the original deal because you will not like anything else."

Max wanted to lunge forward and lock his fingers around her throat. Instead, he clutched Sandra's hand and stared at the ground. "Fine."

"I'm sorry. A little louder, please."

Lifting his head, grinding his teeth, he said, "We have agreed to your terms. You have our promise to support you should you ever rise against Cecily Hull."

"Sandra?"

Sandra's hand tightened. "I agree with my husband. You have our promise."

"Excellent." Madame Ti leaned back onto one elbow. "Meet me tomorrow on Graveyard Island at dusk. I will be prepared to honor my end of this agreement then."

Max and Sandra stood, turned away, and headed toward the exit. They only managed a few steps before Madame Ti cleared her throat.

"I almost forgot — you need to bring J along. He's the one Miller is attached to, so the spell won't work without the boy."

She knew. She knew all along. Max started to turn back but Sandra tugged on his arm. She was right. They needed to get out of there while they still could.

Chapter 10

MAX HATED TO ADMIT IT — loathed to admit it — but he actually felt better now that they had enlisted Madame Ti's help. In the coming day, they would stand on Graveyard Island with a powerful witch who would be able to release Alexander Miller, and in doing so, they would free J from ghostly harm.

Max doubted they would be free from making good on Madame Ti's payment — if anything, by agreeing to support her, she would be encouraged to make a move sooner than later against Cecily Hull — but he could not fight all enemies at once. With their deal in place, he only had to focus on the one enemy for now. And maybe, just maybe, Sandra's growth as a witch would be able to extract them from Madame Ti's grasp at a future date. Somehow.

Max chuckled. *I suppose that's what they call magical thinking.*

But all of that wouldn't begin until the next day. And as Max and Sandra drove J to the Grand Theater multiplex, Max decided to push aside those thoughts for one night. J would soon be having his first date. A great milestone. In the spirit of things, Max decided to take Sandra out for dinner, too. Why should J be the only one to enjoy a date?

"Nervous?" Max asked J.

The young man shifted in his seat and did his best to puff up. "Course not. I'm looking forward to it. If I seem nervous, I'm just thinking a little bit about tomorrow."

"Nothing to be nervous about that. We've handled all kinds of things involving witches and ghosts — trust us. Tomorrow, Miller will be on his way to a better place and you'll be free of his trouble."

Sandra glanced around. "I don't see Private Miller. Is he still bothering you?"

"Not like before. I think Uncle Drummond's been keeping him out of my way. At least, for tonight."

"Well, your Uncle Drummond is one of the good ones."

When they dropped J off, Max wanted to wait and meet this girlfriend, but Sandra insisted they keep moving. J deserved his privacy, and since he had not deigned even to share the girl's name, Sandra thought it best that they leave right away.

With a reluctant grimace, Max drove off.

They traveled all the way down to University Parkway to enjoy a quiet table at Ryan's Restaurant — an upscale steak and seafood place. The cost would hurt their wallets, but Max and Sandra needed a night to themselves. Since they didn't really care about the venue (which looked lovely), or the food (which smelled award-winning), but rather simply wanted a gentle, romantic respite, Max wondered if they should have opted for Wendy's. Then again, being practical at all times could hurt a relationship every bit as much as being carefree at all times.

Sitting at a small table, surrounded by the ambiance of fine dining, they laced fingers and looked into each other's eyes and listened to each other's breath. And for a fleeting few seconds, Max's troubled world vanished. Only her soft smile remained. Only the tickle of her nails on the back of his hands or the rustle of her hair against her collar filled his life. He inhaled her scent and tried to paste this moment into his mental album so that it could be drawn upon any day.

But then he caught that twitch on the corner of her mouth. The real world rumbled back up his spine and tightened around his throat. Sitting back, he buried his head in the menu.

"You're nervous, too?" he said.

She sipped from a glass of wine. Then, forcing a lightness into her tone: "A little, but nothing to be concerned about."

"I can't stop thinking about what we've gotten into. Madame Ti?"

"I know. But our son's safety means more than our own."

The waiter arrived and took their orders before leaving them in peace.

"I have to admit something," Max said, searching for the words. "I've been torn up about this whole case, but I've also allowed us to push forward on it. And I'm starting to think that perhaps it's not just because J is attached with this ghost. I know we failed at breaking this tether, but we've dealt with difficult magic before. I'm sure, given time, we'd find an answer — one that doesn't require Madame Ti in our lives. No, I'm starting to think that part of me secretly likes the whole thing."

"Oh really?"

"Not what Miller's doing, of course, or getting screwed over by Madame Ti, but the rest — I mean, weren't you a little excited when J came to us with this case?"

"Absolutely. That's why I embraced it in the first place. You're the one who's been trying to get out of the whole thing from the start."

"That was before I understood what was really going on. Part of me thinks it's cool that J wants to follow in our footsteps."

Sandra reached under the table and patted his knee. "And part of you is scared out of your wits that someone like Madame Ti's going to take terrible advantage of him."

"Exactly. This is good work that we do, exciting work, but also terrifying work. It seems like J only sees the fun parts. It's spinning my head, though, and I'm only now seeing it. Even our meeting with Madame Ti — I love that stuff. Not making the deal, of course, but working a case, handling the witch world, it's … well, it's fun. But I don't want J to learn the hard way that you can die doing this job."

"We've done pretty good so far. I think we simply have to trust that we've learned enough to protect ourselves and those we love. It also helps to remember that J has his own personal Uncle Drummond looking over him."

Max grinned. "That he does."

After a few minutes of pleasant conversation, Max headed for the restroom. On his way over, he heard a voice that froze him. He must have been mistaken. All the stress had tricked him with an auditory hallucination. He continued on. After using the restroom, he paused near the bar. He swore he heard that voice again. Scanning the dining room, his eyes confirmed his ears.

Standing halfway inside the far wall, Drummond yanked hard on Miller's arm. Their actual words were too muttered to be understood clearly, but the fact that they struggled at that wall told Max everything. Miller would only be in this restaurant, only struggling to stay, for one reason — his tether.

Max looked over the dining room again and spotted the target — J sat at a small table for two. A black girl, pretty with a bright smile and stylish glasses, sat across from him. She wore a charming, modest dress and appeared quite comfortable in this high-caliber restaurant. J, on the other hand, looked nervous and awkward.

Before acting, Max noticed a rush through his body — his nerves prickling and a heavy weight pressing on his chest. He thought he should be angry, but this wasn't anger. J had lied to him and Sandra, had told them he was taking the girlfriend to a movie. He had lied for no reason. Max would not have cared if J preferred a fancy restaurant for a date.

That feeling — disappointment?

Sure, disappointment at being lied to. But as Max watched J and his girlfriend chatting and grinning, he couldn't connect the word *disappointment* with the emotion surging over his skin. When the true word finally came to him, it hit harder than a ghost's icy touch. Betrayal. Max felt betrayed.

Standing by the bar, unsure whether to go end the date and punish J or pretend like he never saw, he noticed Sandra waving him to their table. Of course. She must have seen Drummond, too — the old ghost apparently had pulled Miller outside. In a foggy walk, Max managed to reach his wife without being noticed.

"Sit," she said, gesturing to his food that had arrived. "Eat."

As Max obeyed, he said, "Did you see —"

"You know I did. And I don't understand why he would lie to us, either."

"It's not right. We've never given him any reason to do things behind our back."

"He's also spent the first part of his life on the streets. He trusts us, but this is a new situation for him. When people are confronted with new and scary things, they often revert back to older, more familiar behaviors. Maybe that's what happened here."

Max bit into his steak — exquisite — but then put his fork down. "We can't let this become the precedent. Especially if he wants to be working with the Porter Agency."

"Honey, you need to relax. Remember, it took us a long time to be completely honest with each other. We have to give him a chance."

"That's my point. When we started, the witch community and the Hulls and all of it — they all thought of us as little insignificant players. The mistakes we made with each other, we survived primarily because nobody considered us a threat. But now — that's not true. J will be joining an agency that's already an established piece on the board. Look at our deal with Madame Ti. She knew all about J. She knew he was part of this case without us even saying so. Our enemies are not going to let him make the kinds of mistakes we made. They'll be watching him closely, looking for any misstep so they can capitalize."

Sandra reached over and lifted his chin. Staring directly into his eyes, she said, "It's just a date. He's just a teen. Cut him some slack."

"I don't know if we can."

"At least let him enjoy this moment. We can talk to him later — calmly — on the drive home."

Max glanced across the dining room. J certainly looked pleased. Nervous but pleased. "How did they even get down here?"

"He's a resourceful young man. Besides, if they weren't spending money on the movies, he could afford an Uber to take him and his girl anywhere in the city. Now, please, forget about J, and let's return to our date."

With a bashful grin, Max said, "Sorry. You're right."

"I usually am."

He looked away from J but never made it back to Sandra or a second bite of his steak. Because sitting at the bar, watching J's date with great interest, Max spotted Ruby.

"Son of a —" Max jumped to his feet.

Sandra snapped her attention. "What now?"

But he already stormed over to the bar and stepped in front of Ruby. She had gone with the red wig and lipstick to match. Sipping a gin and tonic, she reminded him of a ladybug — a little hard-shelled insect crawling around like a beetle that could suddenly open its back, flap its unseen wings, and fly off. He had to be careful.

"Well, hey there, Mr. Porter. What a lovely surprise." Thick accent and all smiles again.

Max thrust his hands in his pockets to keep them from grabbing Ruby by the wrists and shaking her. "Looks like Madame Ti didn't understand how serious we were when we said that J was to be left out of this."

"He's going to be at Graveyard Island tomorrow, ain't he?"

"We promised we would be there with him, and we will. There's no need for you to keep an eye on things."

She shrugged. "Some people have a different opinion regarding that."

"Threatening us this way is a stupid mistake. You know, Madame Ti keeps saying that she understands who we are, but you better be careful because I don't think she's right. In fact, I think she underestimates us substantially." He tread in closer. "For your own benefit, you should do a little research, look into our history here. Because people like you — the ancillary people — bad things happen to people like you when everything falls apart."

"You really are cocky."

"Only realistic. We've lasted through several different witch regimes. I've seen what happens, and I'd hate to see that happen to you. You seem like a nice gal. Strange, but nice."

She sat up straighter and peered over his shoulder. "Oh, I get it now. You were the distraction while your wife broke up the sweet little date."

Max did not glance back. There had been no plan. In fact, Ruby's mention of Sandra brought his wife crashing into his mind for the first time since leaving the table. But then, that's part of what made them such a good team. She knew what needed to be done even before he did.

"Don't let any of that fool you. I meant everything I said. You should really consider a different line of work — or at least, a new employer. Madame Ti can only bring you to a bad end."

Ruby eased off the bar stool, dug out a small purse, and laid a hundred-dollar bill on the table. "I'd say I'm doing just fine. See you tomorrow." She walked away. Didn't even wait for the change.

Max hurried back to his table, paid the bill, and joined Sandra and J out by the car. Neither looked happy. Great. Two dates ruined.

Chapter 11

CAUGHT BETWEEN A SEETHING TEENAGER and a scowling wife, Max did his best to keep his attention on the road. But as much as he tried, the harsh exhalations from the backseat and the tapping of ring against window from the passenger seat consistently reeled him back. Then he would remember that he was the parent in this situation, he had done nothing wrong, and he shouldn't be the one in trouble.

"Look," he said, startling his passengers, "I know you're mad at us for ruining your date. I am sorry about that. We had hoped to let it slide until we spoke with you tonight, but the situation changed and we had to act."

"Why?" J said, trying hard not to whine. "What was the big emergency?"

"No, no. We're not shifting the topic. You need to own up to the fact that you lied to us."

"I told you we were going on a date." J crossed his arms and looked out the window. "That wasn't a lie."

"You really want to parse out words like that? This isn't a courtroom. You knew full well that you led us to believe you were taking this girl to the movies. We expected you to be there. And heck, we don't even know her name."

"Her name's Janal. And the rest doesn't make a difference. We were out. We would've been back at the movie theater curb to be picked up. What more do you really need?"

"We need to trust you." Max considered pulling over so he could turn around and face J, but he noticed Sandra pointing ahead with a subtle gesture. He drove on. "You need to understand that we're still your guardians. We're still responsible for you boys. And the scary part you really need to understand

— you can still be taken away from us. Thrown into the system."

With an exasperated slap of his hands against his legs, J said, "It was a date. That's all. We didn't go running off to rob a convenience store, we didn't shoot heroin, or anything. We went out to have dinner."

"And you lied about it."

Sandra put up her hands. "Enough. Both of you. J, you've got to understand that we love you and care about you, that we don't want any harm to come to you. We're not out to ruin your dating life or cramp your style or whatever you call it now, but it's our job to watch out for you and we can't do that effectively if you're lying to us."

"Exactly," Max said.

"Don't get all righteous. You're just as bad."

"What did I lie about?"

"You're not lying, but you're trying to control every aspect of what J does. I know you mean well, that you want to protect him, but these boys are only going to push back if you come at them so hard."

"That's right," J said. "I didn't tell you about the dinner because I knew you'd want to tell me what restaurant to go to and you'd question if this was a good first date for this girl and crap like that. If I gave you the chance, you'd probably have made the reservation and sat at a nearby table to make sure it went okay."

Max cringed. "We didn't intend to be at the same restaurant."

"You see?" J said to Sandra. "He doesn't hear anything I'm saying."

"Well, I'm hearing it all," Drummond said as he appeared in the backseat next to J. "I think every ghost in the Other can hear all of you yammering away."

"Great," Max said. "The peanut gallery's here."

With a flick at the brim of his hat, Drummond said, "Partner, you'll come out of this a whole lot cleaner if you close your mouth and drive. Trust ol' Drummond on this one."

Though Max's eyes flared, he felt Sandra place a hand on his shoulder. It was that calming hand, again, the one that always broke down his defenses. Fine. They all had their little outbursts, and his wife seemed to think that J might respond better to Drummond at the moment. Max had to agree. He didn't like it, but he agreed with it.

Checking the rearview mirror periodically, he caught Drummond looking at J, perhaps waiting for the young man to look back. When J finally did, Drummond ignored the defiant glower. "See, kid, it's like this — everything your folks have said is true, but none of it cuts to real core of it all. The fact is that when Max and Sandra and I go out on a case, we often find ourselves in tricky situations. Dangerous ones. You understand?"

J shrugged.

"It means that we've got to rely on each other to survive. Look, you know that ghosts are real and you know witchcraft is real, too. How do you think, when facing all that, your folks have lived long enough to become your guardian? They do it by trusting each other no matter what happens. That trust then carries over into all aspects of their lives."

"What? I've got to worry about what they're thinking because of their job?"

"Not at all. You want to lie to them, deceive them a little bit, you go right ahead. Thing is, the three of us are under the impression that you want to join in with what we do. It'll be tough for that to happen if we can't trust you. Pretty much impossible. Tomorrow, we're all going to Graveyard Island. Who knows how that'll play out when you've got a witch like Madame Ti along? You'll be facing some real danger, and we need to know that we can count on you. On each other."

J's face softened. "Me? I'm going with you?"

Max said, "Yeah. You were so nervous about your date and about us getting rid of Miller tomorrow, we decided to hold off telling you until afterwards. Never got the chance, though."

"I didn't know I was going along." J's voice rose in pitch. "I'm sorry. I am. I didn't realize, well, any of it. I just thought you were trying to tell me who I can and can't date."

Sandra said, "You know us better than that. You should, at

least."

"I tried to explain to Janal that we should tell you, but she got weird about it. She doesn't have a great relationship with her parents. But I am sorry. I promise I'll do better. I'll be honest and trustworthy and all of that."

"Stop right there," Drummond said, lowering his head so that he gazed down hard at J. "You got two more things to apologize for."

"I do?"

"First off, you lied to your folks, that's between you and them in the long run. But you almost put me in a terrible position. If Max and Sandra had not been at that restaurant to bust you, then you would have expected me to keep this date a secret. You would've wanted me to lie to them. I hope I've made it clear tonight that I won't do that. Ever."

"I got it."

"A little more respect in that answer, please."

"Yes, sir. I'm sorry."

"Second thing, I don't care what your girlfriend said or what she asked you to do. Even if the whole plan was her idea, you be the gentleman. You take the fall."

"Yes, sir."

"Provided she's worth it, of course." Drummond leaned back and clapped his hands together. "Okay. What'd I tell you? Uncle Drummond knows how to handle these things. It's all good."

"I wouldn't go that far," Max said. "But we're on the right road again. Tomorrow, J, you need to trust us. You need to do what we say and tell us the truth no matter what happens."

"Honey," Sandra said. "I think he understands now."

"I do. I do." J clamped his mouth tight. He knew he had dodged a serious punishment. Max could see that much on his face. Hopefully, all of his promises of enlightenment would prove to be more than a teenager's desperate words.

Sandra appeared satisfied with J's change of heart. Perhaps Max should be, too. He would give the boy a chance, that much was certain, but with Madame Ti involved and the risks of an attached ghost, Max refused to be satisfied about any of it.

Chapter 12

THE NIGHT WAS NOT OVER. When they finally reached home, Max planned to slip off his clothes, throw on a T-shirt and some pajama bottoms, and collapse into bed. Instead, he discovered PB sitting at the kitchen table, picking at the splintered center. The table wobbled due to its split legs, and Max knew they would have to buy a new one eventually. When they could afford it.

Watching PB, Max picked up the silent signals right away. Nothing specific, but he could tell by the way PB's eyes followed him, the way PB pretended to be hunched over his schoolwork, the way PB checked the clock over and again — he had been waiting for Max. Once everyone had settled in — Sandra getting ready for bed and J stomping off to the bathroom — PB asked Max for a few minutes.

"You can have as many minutes as you like." Max pulled out a chair.

And then nothing.

PB held still with his hands folded on the table. He stared down. Right before Max's eyes, the boy appeared to shrink, metamorphose into a trembling bit of prey. Only Max had no clue what might be stalking him. School troubles? Bullies? PB could hold his own. Max found it hard to believe anybody at school would mess with him — at least, not more than once.

A flash of inspiration struck. Max walked to the hallway closet, and after a short time rummaging about, he returned with a cheap but serviceable chess set. Staying quiet, he laid out the board and started setting up pieces.

"We need to see who goes first," PB said.

"You can be white and go first. It's been ages since I've

played. Might help to watch your move before I take a turn." They continued to set up the game. Once they finished, and PB led with a center pawn, Max said, "Chess club, huh?"

"Nah. Not anymore."

"It's only been a couple days."

"Yeah, but it's not the same as playing with — well, it's not the same. I didn't really get along with the others."

Max moved a pawn. "I imagine they're a bunch of hardcore players."

"Yeah. Not my kind of thing. I don't mind a good fight, but these guys know every single move you can make. And they've named each one. I just wanted to play some chess and have a good time. Maybe have a group to hang out with. I don't know. It's stupid."

"Not stupid at all. Everybody wants friends to spend time with. If chess isn't the right fit, try something else."

"I'm going to." PB continued to maneuver about the board, gradually taking one of Max's pieces after another. "On Monday, they're having tryouts for the choir. Mrs. Munly said I could probably sing a good bass."

"Singing? You're full of surprises." Max paused to study possible moves but noticed the sly triumph on PB's face. "I've already lost, haven't I?"

"There are a couple ways out that I know, probably a few others, but the way you're playing, I'd say you're done."

Max toppled his King. "You ready to talk? What's bothering you?"

As PB helped clear away the game, the words gushed out. "I don't mean to sound ungrateful or anything, and I'm not trying to get between you and your mother, but she's been teaching me for a long time now and even though you don't always get along, she and I really worked well together, but suddenly she's done with it all and I've got to go to public school and she says she's fine but I know you went to the hospital, so what the hell is going on?"

Max sat back and tried to give his son a comforting, fatherly nod. "She's sick."

"I know that much. She's got MS, right?"

"Yeah. No cure for it, and I think it's strange to develop so late in life. No less deadly, though."

"I get that. I do. And I know that she had to stop teaching — it's a lot of work and exhausting and all that — but I've tried to call her and she either doesn't answer or when she does, it's all short words and the call is over in like a minute. Did I do something to piss her off?"

"Not at all."

"Then what?" PB made a fist but held back from slamming the table. "Doesn't seem right for her to shut me out."

Sitting under the kitchen's hanging lamp felt like an interrogation, but Max couldn't tell who played what role. He wondered if the boy's anger would block any advice he could offer or if it might turn that advice into an accusation, an attack. He considered pushing the conversation aside, promising to talk more in the morning, but rejected the idea. PB would see right through any stalling.

With a sigh, Max said, "As much time as you've spent with my mother, it's not enough to really understand her. Heck, I've known her my whole life, and I barely understand her. But I've learned that if I put on these mental filters to what she says and does, it helps me make sense of her."

"Mental filters?"

"I've never really thought of it so directly, but I'm trying to give you some way to think of them. Like the first filter you have to use is this — understand that everything she does, in her mind, is to protect those she loves. When she stopped homeschooling you and sent you to public school, the first filter to see that through says that she did it so you wouldn't have to watch her suffer through her disease. She thinks she's protecting you from trauma by helping you to avoid it."

"But she could still talk with me."

"The phone thing is a mixture of her desire to protect along with another filter you have to go through — she doesn't acknowledge painful things in her life. She'll jump through Olympic-sized mental hoops to avoid dealing with hard truths.

If she can't avoid them, then she frames it all as a tough love moment, some way of thinking that she's protecting you by saying these hard truths. In your case, she's avoiding you because she knows that you'll eventually ask about her MS and then she'll have to deal with it. With me, she's cold and brutally frank about it all because she knows I've got to handle things for her after she can't do it herself."

Still making fists, PB crossed his arms. "That's stupid. I don't need her protection, and dealing with problems is the only way to get through them."

"I didn't say my mother was right about any of this. I'm letting you know how her mind works. At least, as far as I've been able to figure out."

Max watched PB's fierce scowl and it hit him. PB had only a few close, trusted people in his life. More than any other, he had J. The two had survived the streets together, worked for Max together, and stayed together as Max and Sandra became their guardians. But PB also had Mrs. Porter — even called her *Grandma.* Because she homeschooled him while J went to public school, PB's relationship with her had grown stronger. It was the one relationship PB didn't have to share.

"Tell you what," Max said, pushing out his chair as he stood, "tomorrow morning, I'll take you over to her apartment. You're absolutely right — the two of you need to talk about all of this."

All of PB's anger dissipated, leaving behind a residue of worry. "You should call her first. She's not going to like me just showing up."

"True, but she won't turn you away, either. You can blame me for it, tell her I needed somebody to watch you for the day."

"I can watch myself."

"Tell her whatever you want, but I know this much about her — if you cut off her escape to avoid things, you'll have a better chance of getting through to her. It won't be pleasant, at first — you know she has a sharp tongue — but watching the two of you over the last few years has made something very clear to me. She needs you every bit as much as you need her."

PB tapped a finger on the table. "Maybe I'll bring along my

math homework. She can help me figure it out and that'll make her feel like she's protecting me by helping me through school."

Max gave a firm pat on the shoulder. "Smart move. Now go get some sleep."

Once PB left the kitchen, Max sat alone for a few minutes. He pondered the day's events until he finally found the energy to shuffle into the bedroom. He eased the door open, but Sandra was wide awake, sitting up in bed.

"You okay?" he asked.

"Pretty hard to sleep with tomorrow looming. Ruby spying on our son doesn't help, either. Everything okay with PB?"

Max shared the conversation with his wife. "I know PB is close to my mother — I really do understand it — but I've always worried that at some point, she would do this. Reject him in some way."

"I know."

"He doesn't deserve that. I'm not saying she should be happy about her diagnosis, but she shouldn't take it out on him."

"I know."

"I'd rather she lay into me. Scream all she wants at me. She can say whatever horrible things are in her head, and I'll take it. Let her get all that anger out of her system. But why hurt PB?"

After brushing his teeth, he stretched on the bed. Sandra nestled close with her head on his chest. They stayed quiet and still. Max listened to her breathing and guessed that she listened to his heartbeat.

Eventually, he broke the silence. "I know PB can handle this. Really, I'm just ticked at my mother."

"After all our years together, I've learned that feeling never goes away."

Max laughed. "You'd have been proud of him, listening to how he spoke with me, how he's able to figure out what he wants, what's important to him. It's odd. PB is no longer that kid on the streets I would bring water and breakfast sandwiches. He really is growing up. Changing."

"They both are — PB and J. We're going to have to change, too."

Chapter 13

SATURDAY MORNING ARRIVED with a busy household. Sandra and J stuffed one backpack with everything they could think that might come in handy during a long day away from any main roads — first aid kit, flashlights, extra batteries, snakebite kit, compass, hiking ponchos, several energy bars, flares, and plenty more including sandwiches to cover lunch. After testing the weight of the backpack, heavy but not unbearable, they filled a second pack with basic spellcasting supplies — candles of various colors, a container of salt, a container of chalk, matches, a small knife, a wooden bowl, and Sandra's notes.

"Not bad," J said, feeling the weight of the second pack. "That it?"

"That's it for the packing," Sandra said. "Now you and I are going to spend the rest of the morning making wards to give us a little protection when we're on the island. But don't go thinking you'll be invincible. A ward is good to have but it can be broken. I'm not that great at making them, so mine tend to break easy. Still, it's better than not having one."

Max kissed Sandra and gave J a pat on the back as he walked out the door with PB. That had been several miles and twenty minutes ago. He pulled into his mother's apartment complex and parked. His fingers griped and released the steering wheel as if he gave the car a deep massage while PB sat next to him.

"I'll be fine," PB said. "I know how I sounded last night, but I'm thinking better this morning. I'm used to Grandma Porter, and I know how to talk to her. She'll snip a lot, of course, but by dinnertime tonight, she'll open up to me."

"You've got it all figured out, huh? Good for you. I never got the hang of dealing with her. Not like you, anyway."

"She's not my mom. Not my parent. I call her *Grandma* but really, she's more like a friend. It's a lot easier to be tough with a friend." PB put his hand on the door but did not leave. "You'll probably do better with J if you think of him like that. Like a friend."

Max frowned. "I'm not tough enough on him?"

"That's not what I'm saying. Your problem is that you think of him like your son."

"He is my son. You are, too."

"I know. And I've come to see you as my dad. But J's not quite there yet. This whole thing is not normal — you understand that, right? You and Sandra helping us, taking us off the streets, becoming our guardians — that's not normal. Back before we met you, if one of our friends got approached by a nice couple that wanted to take care of them, we knew that was bad news. It either meant something to do with drugs or prostitution. If it wasn't those two, then it got real dark, and we didn't want to know about it. You'd hear stories and those were worse than any urban legend you can bring up."

Max pursed his lips as he thought this over. "That ever happen to you or J?"

"No way. We were too smart for that. It's why when we started with y'all, it was strictly a business deal. Only later it became more than that, and by then, we knew we had a good thing going with you two. But to jump from that to seeing you as his daddy — that's a big leap."

"You made it."

"Only because my birth-dad showed up and nearly killed me in the process."

"Yeah, there's that. But J seemed more accepting of the idea than you."

"He wasn't into girls back then, either. Things change."

"I'm not trying to force him to be my son. I think of him that way, but it's not required that he reciprocate. I just want him to be safe."

PB opened the door and glanced back. "Best thing you can do is give him space. When it was the two of us, I kind of saw myself as his father. Nah, more like his big brother. I felt responsible for him, y'know? I learned quick that I got more from not pushing him than pushing. But hey, that's what it was like for me. Maybe it's different with you because you're so much older."

Max laughed. "Real nice."

"Call it like it is, old man."

After seeing PB enter the apartment building, Max drove home. Stepping into the living room, he found Sandra and J crouched in the middle of a chalk casting circle on the floor. They had constructed two wards already and worked on a third. Drummond hovered near the bookshelves and tipped his hat towards Max — he was in the middle of a story and clearly did not want to stop his flow.

"It was at that point that I realized what really had been going on in apartment 2A, and knowing that, I could make a plan for how to get out of that building. Because that ghost was one of the meanest I ever dealt with."

Sandra said, "Don't exaggerate. J has enough to worry about with his own ghost problems."

"That's why I'm telling this. If you'd let me finish, you'd understand that even as tough as that case was, I eventually helped the ghost — granted, a few people got hurt on the way, and I suffered a bit myself — but I did get out. That's the point, J. You'll get out of this, too. Don't worry."

"That's right," Max said. "You've got nothing to worry about. Not when the three of us are with you."

He wanted to say something more hopeful, more inspiring, but he figured his body language would betray him if given the chance. Still, J gazed up at him with an eager face. That chilled Max's bones.

"Listen," he said, squatting next to J, "I'm glad you're excited about this, and it's a good thing if you're nervous, too, but you've got to keep a clear head. That's always the most important thing on a case. Keep your head clear and pay attention. The little details are often the ones that break out the truth."

"The truth?" J said. "There ain't no big secret to uncover. We go there, cast the spells, and I'm done with the guy. Isn't that it?"

"With any luck. I'll even cross my fingers for you. But it's been our experience that these things never go easy. And if they start off easy, watch out. That's when the real bad stuff is going to happen."

"Bad stuff?"

Sandra said, "Stop it. J's got enough on his mind. He doesn't need your worries, too. I swear the two of you are going to give this boy a stroke with all your helpful advice."

Max stood, his mouth open to retort, but he held back. No matter how much he wanted to emphasize the dangers, nothing he could say would change anything. He waited until they completed the third ward. Then he simply said, "Let's go."

Chapter 14

BY THE TIME MAX DROVE TO WHITNEY and found his way onto Old Whitney Road, the afternoon had begun to wane. The recent rains had kept the sky a gloomy gray, so as dusk approached, the world simply altered from bland to dark. Sandra had spent much of the trip sharing stories with J detailing their successful cases involving ghosts, and through each telling, she managed to soften or avoid any of the gritty details. Drummond and Miller floated in the back, both halfway out of the car so as not to crowd J. At least, that was how Sandra conveyed it — from Drummond's grumbling, Max got the sense Miller was not accommodating. When they finally arrived, Max parked off a side road next to the railroad tracks and popped the trunk.

Shouldering one of the backpacks and handing the second to Sandra, he said, "There's no road access, no plumbing, no electricity, nothing much in the way of lighting — basically nothing but empty land and dead people. We have to stay close. No wandering off."

Whitney may have been a thriving town once or maybe it always had been a quaint but healthy village. That had been the past. Now, it had become a rural outpost for people who abhorred the city. The homes were varied from trailers to modular to custom made, but each sat on a sizeable chunk of land covered with old trees. It was one of those dying areas in America where the rich and poor lived side by side, and it wasn't always clear who was who.

With a bounce in his step, J headed for the tracks. Pleased he didn't have to say a word, Max watched as Drummond hovered close to the boy. Miller also stayed nearby, according to Sandra, but that did less to make Max feel comfortable.

"He's not going to try anything," she said. "Not when there's a chance he'll be set free."

"Yeah, but if this doesn't work, especially after more than a century, I'm not so certain he'll just shrug and calmly remain attached to J without ever bothering our son again. What's really scary — if that ghost becomes angry, he might lose all sense of himself. He might become a poltergeist. Then we'll have a problem far worse, and J —"

"J will be fine. Drummond's here to stop Miller from anything like that."

From the tracks, J bounced along, calling back, "C'mon, you two. Let's get moving."

The path ran straight and long. Overgrowth rose on either side of the rails, sometimes reaching up and across in an attempt to form a tunnel. Every so often they hiked by a sign stapled into the bark of a tree — NO TRESSPASSING. Birds fluttered above and some sang of the ending day, but otherwise, Max noticed a lack of wildlife. Off to the left, Badin Lake underscored the observation by offering an eerie, still view. Quiet. Like a solid sheet of marble that no one walked upon.

Max pictured the town drowned below — the houses, the church, the streets and street signs, the pharmacy and old-time barber shop, the elementary school with a playground in the back that would be seen as a deathtrap by today's standards. And that World War II bomber. Probably some other horrors as well — bodies dumped by mobsters or cars sunk to dispose of evidence. Possibly some somber events, too — an engagement ring thrown into the lake when the wedding was called off or the ashes of a loved one who wished to be returned to the waters.

A steep hill formed on the left, blocking the view of the lake, and J scurried up to the top. He made a short circle and hastened back to the tracks. "More of the same," he said. "How much longer do we have to hike?"

"We haven't been hiking long," Max said. "A few hours to go, I'm guessing. We should arrive right around when we're supposed to be there."

Later, they came across a low wall made of railroad ties — thick, heavy slabs of wood stacked alongside the track. Weeds and vines had taken over the ordered pile making it clear that nobody had bothered with this area in quite a while. Nature attempted to reclaim as much as she could, slowly transforming the once active line into wild lands again. Except Max got the sense that the trains still rumbled down this way — albeit infrequently.

Another hour went by. Despite the overcast day and the lowering sun, they still ended up sweating. After guzzling a water bottle dry, Sandra wiped her forehead and said, "Drummond, will you be a sweetheart and scout ahead? We should be reaching the island soon, and I'd rather not have any unpleasant surprises."

Drummond peered down the tracks, then glanced back at J and Miller. "Normally, I wouldn't hesitate — especially for you — but I don't like the idea of leaving any of you back here with Miller around. Or the other ghosts, for that matter."

"Other ghosts?" Max said.

Softly, J said, "They've been coming by a little at a time. Staring at us and then drifting away. Two are here right now."

"More soldiers?"

"No. There's an old lady by that tree. She's bent over and has a scarf around her head. There's also a guy laying across the tracks. Looks drunk and homeless."

Max noticed Sandra had walked around the section of track J had pointed out. "Give them all plenty of space. Don't let me walk through any of them."

"Just follow me and Sandra. You'll be fine."

Turning his attention toward Drummond, Max said, "What about Miller? Any changes in his behavior?"

Drummond appraised the air to his right. "Nothing really different. Still can't understand what he's saying. If anything, I'd say he's figured what we're going to do — more or less — and I don't think he wants to rock the boat."

"That may be, but let's not expect a near-crazed ghost to become a peace-loving teddy bear."

After another half-hour, the narrow strip of land that had been their path the entire time opened up to a wide section of old trees, dead leaves, and plenty of rocks. "Is this it?" Sandra asked. "Are we on the island?"

Max checked the GPS in his phone. Without any roads or buildings, the map program did not want to cooperate with exact placement, but it was close enough. "Looks like it. The first graveyard should be further in and off to the right."

As they approached the area, Drummond tipped his hat and greeted the various ghosts surrounding them. Sandra's face blanked and paled. Same way she always looked when they went to a cemetery or hospital or anyplace that had too many ghosts. J, however, looked about with wide-eyed fascination like a kid on a Disney ride.

Sandra pulled him aside but spoke in a firm voice that Max could easily hear. "These are not playthings. They were once living people, and now, most of them are lost or hurting. Ghosts like Drummond are the exceptions. You have to be careful. You don't want to have another one of these things attach to you. Or worse."

"What do I do to stop that?" J said, snatching peeks at all the paranormal sights.

"Try not to stare at them, for one. Don't gawk. Don't engage with them. If they talk to you, try not to be rude but don't let them lure into a conversation. Ghosts at graveyards can be volatile. Think of them like sharks. As long as we don't challenge any of them, as long as we don't advertise ourselves as tasty morsels, they'll leave us alone. But if we get them excited, it'll be like a feeding frenzy. And if that happens, you've got your ward."

Max listened to all Sandra said and wondered if she had exaggerated the threat to scare J. Not that he doubted her, but rather, much of what she said did not connect with his own experiences dealing with the dead in graveyards. Then again, he had the benefit of not being able to see any of them. Perhaps the rules changed when facing them directly.

While Sandra continued to speak with J, Max strode into the first graveyard. From his research, he knew what to expect — thought he did, anyway — but that had not truly prepared him. The place looked nothing like a respected land for the dead. If anything, it appeared to be a swath of unused forest where bodies had been dumped. The graves were scattered about — Max expected that would be the case — but they were in such haphazard clusters that the headstones were no more than odd rock formations.

One headstone perched midway on a hill with a fallen log cutting it off from two more further below struck his interest. All three stones came up to the knees. Simple designs — nothing more than a slab with a gentle arch at the top. Moss and vines had to be cleared away in order to read the inscriptions, and on two of them, Max found the writing had worn off to the point of being illegible. That would be a common problem with these older headstones. They were made from limestone which dissolved under polluted rain. With his phone he snapped a few pictures and double-checked that each one would be copied into the Cloud.

A chill crossed his skin. Pulling at vines on one headstone, he did his best to ignore the cold. If he thought about it too long, if he acknowledged that a ghost had drifted through him, another chill would prickle his body — one that could lead to panicked thinking. Just because he had dealt with ghosts on numerous occasions did not mean he could fight off his natural instincts forever. The human body was hardwired to avoid the cold of death. Heck, even a touch of Drummond's frosty air could shudder Max's nerves. He should focus on taking pictures. Documenting everything.

Glancing at Sandra, it hit Max that she hated hospitals and cemeteries for this reason, too. He always thought it was just seeing all the dead, hearing them, being crowded by them, and that was true. Gruesome visages and painful moans tended to ruin anybody's day. But now he thought that she probably had to struggle against the same instincts he did, except on a far greater level. After all, he only felt the chill. She could see the threats all around them.

Focus. He needed to find Miller's grave. The sooner they put that dead soldier to rest, the sooner they could all leave the island.

Moving across to a cluttered section of five graves, Max spotted Drummond chatting with the air. The old ghost pointed in one direction but was corrected and looked off in another. With a nod of appreciation, he headed away. Max didn't think his partner would be any more successful, though. If the ghosts on this island knew where to find Miller's headstone, they would have already helped out their old friend. After all, they should remember him from spending over a decade hanging out in the original cemetery before the creation of Badin Lake.

Max inspected headstone after headstone and continued sending photos into the Cloud. The family names did not cluster together and the burial dates covered far reaching times with abandon. Here he found Abagail West 1802 - 1854. There he found Phineas Gruft 1887 - 1917. And next door was Robert Connor 1823 - 1900.

Looking around, however, Max discovered too many headstones that could not be deciphered. Many had eroded but some were damaged by falling trees or the ravages of heavy storms. Some had been vandalized. He did find evidence of parties — empty beer cans, crumpled bags of chips, and a few condom wrappers.

No witchcraft, though. No forgotten candles, no marked graves, no symbols carved into tree trunks. Nothing to suggest that witches regularly utilized the ghosts on this island. Like the town below the water, the island had become a corpse of its own.

At least, Max thought of it that way until he noticed the lone headstone situated back from any others. It had been placed under a maple tree and furry vines crept up one side of the stone — poison ivy. Max pulled out his phone and zoomed the camera image onto the headstone. With flourishing swoops to the lettering, it read: *Delilah French 1792 - 1892 May her soul find the rest she never did in her hundred years.* Under this sorrowful epitaph, the stone had been chipped away by a less-skilled hand.

"Sandra, over here," Max called. When she stepped up next to him, he pointed out the markings. "Am I wrong or are those witch symbols?"

She took hold of his phone and concentrated. "They are. But the intention is not really easy to spot. Maybe they're trying to keep Ms. French's ghost from leaving the island. Or maybe they wanted her to regain her strength as fast as possible."

"Regain from what?"

"Dying. She was a hundred years old. She could probably use a little pep once she returned."

"Do we know that she did return?"

"I don't know anything about her. Never heard of her."

Max gestured toward Drummond. "What about you? You ever hear about Delilah French?"

Pushing his hat back, Drummond said, "Can't say that I have. But there have been thousands of witches I've had to deal with in my time. Ms. French probably never met me, or she would have made a bigger impression."

Staring at the headstone, feeling its cold wrap around him like all the ghosts drifting across the island, Max snapped another picture. A buzzing noise grew louder in the distance. Turning back, Max saw J walking toward the water.

Drummond shot off to be near the boy, and while that quick maneuver propped up Max's confidence in his team, he couldn't help the spear of terror that pierced through him. Seeing J walking off made Max want to scream out as if watching a toddler ambling toward a busy road.

Before he could summon a word, however, he saw J halt and give a tentative wave toward the lake. Drummond floated nearby, and as Max and Sandra joined up, a small motorboat zipped into view. Madame Ti sat on the cushioned bench near the front while Ruby, sporting black hair slicked back, operated the boat. They pulled alongside a broken dock and Ruby assisted Madame Ti out.

Dressed in all black, including a wide-brimmed hat with a short veil hanging off the edges, Madame Ti walked straight toward the group. She inclined her head at the space next to

Drummond as if listening to a bird. With single nod, she said, "Mr. Miller, I am here to help you." She looked over the Porter Agency. "Let us begin."

Chapter 15

MADAME TI SCRUTINIZED RUBY'S CARE in bringing a leather satchel over to the team. Max watched both women, ready for any sudden movement, any change in the expected plan. But that was silly. He knew better. These women weren't mobsters or petty criminals. They were witches. And a witch, especially the head witch of North Carolina, would not succeed in controlling all the spellcasters in the state — an anarchic and powerful group — by breaking her word.

Still, Max thought it best to remain vigilant.

"Have you located Private Miller's headstone?" Madame Ti asked.

"Not yet," Max said. "Considering the condition these graves are in, I'm not confident we will find it."

"Oh, we will." She folded her hands in front like a demure lady and turned toward Sandra. "Good to see you again. I'm looking forward to producing some magic together." Shifting to one foot, Madame Ti leaned slightly to look at the young man standing further back. "You must be J. You've certainly caused a bit of trouble for everybody, haven't you?"

Sandra stepped over to block J from view. "You'd do best to limit your interactions with our son. He's only here because he has to be for the spell to work."

"And you'd do best to remember that you are not in charge here. If I want to converse with your son, then I will do so."

"Hey," J said, and all eyes turned toward him. "You want to talk to me, that's fine. As long as you get this ghost taken care of. But don't go bullying Sandra."

Madame Ti exchanged an impressed look with Ruby. "A bit of a spark. A little older and he'd be perfect for you."

Hiding her blush beneath a stern bodyguard attitude, Ruby clasped her hands behind her back and stared straight ahead.

Max said, "Are we waiting for anything else, or can we get started?"

With a glance at the sky, Madame Ti gestured in Sandra's direction. "You'll find everything you need in the satchel. Use the black candle, of course. You'll also find a railroad spike and some twine. Put the spike at the center point and use the twine stretched out to produce a perfect circle large enough to fit us both. It must be perfect, so keep the twine taut as you mark the edges. Then shorten the twine and repeat to make a smaller inner-circle. Leave enough room between the two for clear writing. Understood?"

Sandra said, "Sure. You want a standard casting circle."

"No. I want a perfect casting circle. Every aspect of casting a spell affects the outcome. Too many witches fail to understand that. Sloppy writing, an imperfect circle — these things can destroy a spell's full success. Proper execution of the basics is every bit as crucial as the right pronunciations or the proper mental focus. And when I see how sweet and innocent your young man is, I should think you want the best chances for success you can get."

Max saw the fire rise in his wife and set his foot back, ready to lunge between the two women should it be necessary. But Sandra pulled back from responding and instead walked over to the bag to get what she needed for the circle.

"This will take a little time," Madame Ti said to the others. "Please stay out of our way."

Everyone spread out as Sandra pounded the stake into the ground — perhaps with more vigor than required. Madame Ti brought out a large book with a metal clasp locking it shut.

"You try stealing that book and you're a dead man," Ruby said as she strolled next to Max. When she reached him, she stood like before — legs spread in a firm, stiff stance and arms behind her back, clasped at the elbows.

"What?" Max looked as if he ate the sourest lemon.

"You heard exactly what I said. My job is to protect that

woman, and I'm good at my job. You should ask around. Find out who I am. You'll see you don't want to mess with me."

"Throwing my words back at me? Cute."

"I'll throw you into the lake and keep your head underwater if you cross me. I wonder how *cute* you'll think that is."

Max grinned at her. "I like the ruby-haired Ruby better."

Sandra had tied one end of the string to the stake and walked off several steps. With a sturdy branch, she marked a circle, keeping the string taut. Madame Ti set the book on the ground, used a tiny key to unlock the clasp, and searched through its pages with gentle care.

J meandered by a tree that had fallen into another tree. He had seen casting circles before. Watching two witches build an intricate one could not hold his attention. Instead, he climbed the angled tree a bit — not too high, thankfully — and kicked around the dirt. *Good,* Max thought. Just because J was a teen who had started dating did not remove the kid inside him. Not yet, anyway.

"I don't see why you care about him so much," Ruby said.

"He's my son." Max's incredulity drenched every word.

"Not really."

"Yes, really."

"I mean that you didn't —"

"I know what you meant, but you're wrong to think it. I love that boy more than his biological parents ever did."

"That's sweet. But still —"

"No. There's no *but still* anything. Making a baby does not make a parent. Sandra and I are J's parents. We're the ones showing up each day, doing the hard work, making the decisions." He paused to check Ruby's stoic face. "Did you not have real parents? Did you grow up on the streets, too, but nobody came to help you build a life?"

"Watch it, Porter. Helping build a life does not make it a permanent life."

"You touch that boy, and I'll end yours."

She turned her hard eyes upon him. "I was talking about you."

"You make a lot of threats. That's not a smart thing to do."

"Believe me, I have no problem carrying any of them out."

Drummond drifted closer. "Need a hand?"

Max said, "Well, Ms. Ruby, let me show the kind of threats the Porter Agency can make."

Though Drummond rolled his eyes, he played along. A swipe of his dead hand across Ruby's back curled her over with cold. A breath later, Ruby retreated. She stood alone by a few gravestones and observed the witches, slowly returning to her firm stance and stoic glare. But her right eye twitched as she snatched glances at the empty spaces around her.

"Thanks," Max said.

"Anytime." Drummond watched J picking at some rocks. "He's going to be okay. You'll see."

Max wanted to share his partner's confidence, but his mind brought up image after image of his own perilous encounters over the years. From being handcuffed to basement pipes to risking his life in a haunted brothel, from battling a ghost locked in a loop of death and despair to thwarting cultists bent on controlling magic, from being a pawn of the Hull family to a pawn of the Mobley coven to a pawn of the Magi — throughout it all, Max and Sandra had fought hard and always risked losing. But in their world, *losing* meant more than money, power, or simply embarrassment. *Losing* meant death.

"We're ready," Sandra said, and everyone drew in near.

Madame Ti asked Ruby to remove the stake from within the circle. Sandra cleared away the books and set a wide-based black candle at the northern point. Madame Ti then entered the circle and knelt before the candle like a penitent seeking forgiveness — head bowed, hands clasped in front.

"Isn't this a bit much for a location spell?" Max asked Sandra when she walked over to him.

"Absolutely. But this isn't a mere location spell. We're trying to find two graves for the same man — the one in the island which is empty and the one at the bottom of the lake which has no headstone and is, well, at the bottom of the lake. We also lack anything connected to Miller. If we had a piece of cloth, a handwritten letter, anything that he had touched while living, this detailed casting circle wouldn't be required. But without any of that, Madame Ti is going to rely on Miller's ghostly form itself — draining off bits of the ghost to use as the location connector."

Madame Ti lit the candle, and as she wafted the flickering heat over her face, she recited the spell in its original language — a series of words Max did not know and never would. She then arched her head back, holding still. A breeze rustled the leaves. All else remained quiet.

Setting his phone to silence, he snapped a few pictures of the casting circle. Sandra frowned at him, but he whispered, "We lost all your books in the fire. All those spells are gone. Might as well start rebuilding when we can."

With a gentle smile, she kissed his cheek.

"There," Madame Ti said, pointing off into the woods.

Squinting, Max swore he saw a glowing amber light. Sandra moved first, and the rest followed — all except Madame Ti who remained in the casting circle. With the sun nearly set, the glow grew stronger. It brought them closer like a beacon in the fog, transforming the haphazard graveyard into a warm, inviting cove of light.

Max knew from his research that they had left the first graveyard and entered the second. In an area he thought of as the back corner, they found the headstone, shining bright as if ten bulbs had been placed inside the stone and flicked on simultaneously.

"We've got it," Max called out.

Madame Ti must have heard because the light went out.

Shining a flashlight on the headstone, Sandra said, "Can you read it at all?"

Max brought his face right up to the stone. Small groves marked where the name and dates had once been. Long gone now. But the epitaph remained. *"Though filled with regret, he was loved by all."*

"That's a strange one," Drummond said as he turned to the emptiness on his right. "Why'd you want that on your grave?"

"What did he say?"

With a shake of her head, Sandra said, "He claims it was his wife's idea. He didn't want anything at all, but his wife was the one who always pestered him about getting right with the Lord. He says that she thought his crimes during the war would stop him from getting into Heaven with her."

"What crimes? I know he was in the Confederacy, but I didn't find evidence that he owned slaves or killed Union soldiers or anything. He was just a kid who ended up on the wrong side because of where he was born. I didn't find anything that would be called a war crime or a non-war crime. Nothing like that."

Drummond gestured at Miller. "Well, what about it?" After a few seconds, he turned back to Max. "The guy ain't talking."

Ruby walked up to them carrying a duffel bag. Max hadn't noticed her slip away to the boat to retrieve this bag and chastised himself for the error. From the look on Sandra's face, she had missed Ruby leaving, too.

Tossing the duffel on the ground, Ruby said, "If you're done pretending to chat with ghosts, it's time to dig."

J said, "Lady, just because you don't see something don't make it pretend."

"And just because I look like a small lady doesn't mean I can't snap your neck."

"Hey," Max said. "Watch it."

Ruby grabbed a shovel out of the bag and thrust it at Max. She pulled out two more and handed one to J. "We dig. Now."

As they got to work, Sandra joined Madame Ti to prepare a new casting circle. With nothing to do directly, Drummond patrolled the work area, occasionally stopping by Miller — or where Max thought Miller was — and occasionally chatting up the local ghosts.

In short order, sweat dribbled down Max's back as he plunged his shovel into the hard earth over and over. Ruby and J worked a steady rhythm, and when the sun was gone, they had managed about four feet down. Max climbed out of the grave and opened a bottle of water.

"You're taking all this well," Ruby said to J.

Before Max could warn Ruby off, J said, "Ain't my first time in a graveyard with the Porters. I know you see them treating me like I've never done any of this, but they've brought me along on cases before. Usually just part of it, but I see more than they realize."

"Really? Didn't they ever teach you not to talk with a witch?"

"You ain't a witch."

Ruby glanced up at Max. "Some kid you've got here. You better watch out or he'll have your job before the night's over."

Max tossed J a bottle of water. To Ruby, he said, "I told you not to talk to him. Last chance. Do it again, and I'll have Drummond ice your brain so hard you'll be unconscious for two days."

Raising her hands, she said, "Okay, okay. No need to get all Rambo on me."

"Hey, Max," J said as he crumpled the plastic bottle and tossed it aside. "How come we have to dig this grave? We know it's empty."

"First, pick up your trash. As for the grave, we have to make sure that it is empty — the headstone might be in the wrong spot. But even if everything is fine, we still need to dig the hole so that we have a place to bury Miller once we get his bones."

As J climbed out, retrieved the discarded bottle, and used a trash bag they had brought along, he said, "In that case, let's at least have Drummond check below for bodies. I don't want to disturb anybody down there. I got enough trouble with one ghost attached to me."

"Smart kid," Ruby said.

Max returned to digging while Drummond did as requested. When he came back, he simply said, "All clear." Then he resumed patrolling.

At length, they finished their strenuous work and sat around waiting on the witches. The air grew colder. Max knew it was simply the temperature dropping with the night, but he couldn't help thinking that ghosts were passing through him.

Finally, Sandra said, "I think that's it."

Madame Ti traced the circle with her flashlight before nodding. "Yes. We can begin."

Another chill struck Max, yet he knew exactly where this one came from.

Chapter 16

IF ONE HAD ASKED MAX PORTER, before he ever moved to North Carolina, how many times he would watch witches cast spells, the answer would have been a laugh and the number zero. Since moving to North Carolina, however, Max had witnessed more acts of witchcraft than he ever thought appropriate — no laugh this time but a wish that number was also zero. And while the process of creating a casting circle, lighting the candles, writing the symbols, and chanting the strange words had become a bit routine, he still found the hairs on his arms standing. He still felt a twist in his gut and a hard lump in his throat. He wondered if he would ever become so complacent that even those simple reactions would go away. But he knew the answer. No. For no matter how many times he observed a witch cast a spell, there were no guarantees on the results. Madame Ti's concentration reminded him of this fact as she stretched her arms out like wings and recited the spell's intricate words.

The lengthy phrase took a full minute to say before repeating — unusual for a spell. Normally, the words were few and recurred like a constant echo. They would be said over and again until they melded into a drone like a mantra.

J had seen spells cast before, yet Max noticed how intently the boy watched the proceedings. Even Drummond appeared more interested than usual. It wasn't just the clear difficulty of the spell or its uniqueness. Max suspected the others shared his fascination due in part to Madame Ti's performance.

She did more than simply stand there and speak the spell. She interpreted it. The words, though long dead and unknown to Max, took on meaning from the way she uttered each syllable. He watched an artist at the height of her craft.

Off to the right, somewhere in the still waters of Badin Lake, bubbles rose sounding like the wheezing of an old man as they broke the surface. Max heard them and knew right away they were a result of Madame Ti's spell. No natural cause could create that strange sound.

But the wheezing bubbles died down.

"It's not enough," Madame Ti said, waving Sandra over to help.

Without hesitation, Sandra stepped into the circle and joined hands with Madame Ti. She closed her eyes and lowered her head. Though she did not make a sound, her addition in strength and energy shined clearly when Madame Ti resumed. The words — every bit as foreign as before — became something more. Whereas before they were a script performed by an actress of great skill, the words now became a haunting music, a performance with more than one artist.

The bubbling returned. Stronger than before. And an amber glow pulsed beneath the slick glass of the water. No ripples. No break in the surface. Only the sound of wheezing and the sight of the deep glow.

Sandra groaned and winced as if being struck. Her breathing weakened. "Something's fighting back. Trying to break our spell."

J rushed over to Max. "What do we do?"

"We have to wait," Max said. "Trust them. They'll let us know if we can help somehow."

"But it's hurting her."

"Which is why we have to be ready to do whatever they ask."

Orange sparks danced along the edge of the casting circle like firecrackers. The flashes of light strobed the trees creating gnarled shadows. Max peeked at the lake. The glow had dimmed.

Madame Ti's eyes opened wide. "We can't hold this."

"Don't you quit," Sandra said. "Everybody into the circle. Join hands."

Max and J raced forward, jumping close to Sandra and linking hands. Drummond swept ahead but pulled up short of the circle. He dared put out his hand, and an arc of energy thrust him back.

"Worth a try," he muttered.

Ruby sauntered over, but at least, she did as asked. When she finally clasped Madame Ti's hand, the power surged through all of them.

Max's head wrenched back and his vision blurred. He no longer felt as if he stood in the woods but rather cold water covered his skin. Dark, murky water. He breathed out and air bubbles rose toward the surface.

Swim, kick, push up toward the air, toward the living, Madame Ti said, although it wasn't her voice in his ear. Rather he felt the words coming from her, through her hands, across the circle of people trying to share their energy. Stranger still — part of him knew she spoke in that forgotten witch tongue yet he understood her meaning.

As Madame Ti continued to urge that he swim upward, another odd sensation overcame his body — that it wasn't his body alone. He was Sandra and J and Ruby and even Madame Ti. They were a single force drawing up from the depths, striving for the freedom above the lake. Amber light glowed around them, glittering against particles in the water.

And with a gasping lungful of air, they breached the surface.

Max gazed across the water at the flashlights in the woods. But before he could see himself standing in the distance, his perception ripped away and returned to his body. He held hands in the casting circle once again. Everyone looked at each other with a shared sense of awe.

"Thank you," Sandra said, sweat glistening on her brow. "We can handle this now. Get ready to do the rest."

Max, J, and Ruby released their hands and left the circle. J stared out at the lake, and Max followed his focus — a pile of bones, including a skull and tatters of clothing, floated across the water. Not on it like driftwood, but an inch above the surface like a ghost itself. It pulsed amber light, but this light did not reflect on the water or upon the trees. It was a light made of death that few could perceive.

The bones gently passed over the land as they made a slow path toward the open grave. Max and Ruby picked up their shovels and waited by the pile of dirt they had dug up. As the bones lowered into the hole, J's attention turned toward Drummond.

"Did it work?" J asked.

"Almost, kid." Drummond gestured toward the empty space that should still have been Miller. "He's looking clearer, don't you think?"

"Yeah. Maybe even a little happy."

When the bones finally touched the bottom, Max and Ruby started filling in the grave. Sandra walked over, panting as if she had run several miles. "Looks like the tether is gone. Drummond? J? You see any of it?"

"Nothing," J said. "I don't feel it, either."

"Doll, you did a great job."

As Max continued dumping dirt into the hole, he snatched glances at Sandra. He knew her worried look and did not welcome seeing it at that moment. "Something wrong, hon?"

"Miller's still here. I thought he'd move on right away."

"Maybe we have to finish with the grave first."

"That must be it." She did not sound convinced.

Drummond lowered his head as if in a secret conversation. "I know you've been stuck here for a very long time, but it's all over now. You're free. You can move on and join all your family, your friends, your fellow soldiers. They're all waiting for you." He paused a moment, then looked back and shrugged. "He's not leaving."

Max tossed in another shovelful of dirt. "What do you mean? Why did he make us go through all of this if he didn't want to move on?"

"Oh, he certainly does," Madame Ti said, strolling toward them with enough arrogance and menace to shudder Max's stomach. "He simply can't."

Sandra put a hand on J's shoulder and nudged him away from Madame Ti. "What did you do?"

"I assure you that I've done nothing more than you asked of me. We raised Miller's bones and have put them to rest."

Stepping in front of J, Sandra went on, "But you did

something else. Wait — no, you didn't. But you knew something. I see it in your eyes. You even said it when we first approached you."

"Did I?"

"You said that it was all done the moment we walked in. You knew then that you wanted to be here, wanted to raise these bones. Why, though? What's special about Miller?"

As Max listened to this, he kept an eye on Ruby. If she tried to make a move toward Sandra, he would tackle her to the ground. Just beyond Ruby, Max noticed Drummond shifting into a similar position. Good to know his partner had the same thoughts.

But then it all changed.

The empty space near Drummond no longer was empty. Max could see the pale shape of a lanky young man standing awkwardly. He wore a Confederate uniform and looked frightened as if standing on the precipice of battle. The more that shape could be discerned, the more details Max could see, the more nervous he became. Because this ghost did not glow a pale blue or a clean amber. This ghost glowed purple. No, not a ghost — an inhuman spirit.

Max's heart dropped as if he had entered freefall. His legs wobbled. It had been almost a year since he first dealt with an inhuman spirit, and the thing had nearly destroyed Drummond. Getting rid of it, banishing it through a vortex created by a spell, came close to killing Sandra. And it did manage to burn their office to the ground.

These purple horrors were supposed to be rare. Yet here one floated.

"What is that?" Ruby asked, a slight tremor in her throat.

J stepped closer to Sandra. "Why can the lady see that?"

"All can see it," Madame Ti said. She moved in smooth, ghostly steps. And she laughed. "You'll soon see more."

Max's heart thumped harder. Before he could question the idea of more, three strands of purple appeared — each one stretching out of Miller's purple form. They snaked across the graveyard, through trees and rocks, until they reached three other ghosts. Like Miller, these ghosts were young men, soldiers of the Civil War, and like Miller, they each were now visible to Max. They all glowed purple.

A gleeful laugh burst from Madame Ti. "Come to me, Wardarit. Let me help you."

Wardarit? Max shivered. The witch knew the spirit's name. This was bad. Very bad.

"Max," Drummond said as if he had been saying it several times already. "Get out of here."

Max managed a nod. He caught Sandra's terrified gaze and J's confused look. Finding some force in his lungs, he shoved out one word that snapped them all into action.

"Run!"

Chapter 17

BLASTING BETWEEN SANDRA AND J, Max grabbed their hands as he bolted across the uneven ground. Adrenaline pumped his awareness into ultra-clarity. He saw Madame Ti's delight, Ruby's stoic acceptance, and the anguished purple ghosts tethered together by an inhuman spirit.

"I can run on my own," J said, yanking his hand loose.

"No," Max said, his voice constricted by his fear.

As if smelling chum in the waters, a purplish sphere rose off one of the ghosts.

"Quick, quick," Sandra said, reaching for J's hand. "Those purple things are inhuman spirits and they're repelled by faith in something stronger than yourself. Unless you've suddenly found religion, you need to have faith in us — your family."

The ball of energy shot across the graveyard. J leapt into Sandra's arms as the purple light zipped by them. It did not return to its ghost, however. Not yet. It waited, hovering nearby, searching for a crack in the Porters' armor.

"What do we do?" J said, white-knuckling Sandra's hand.

Drummond soared into view with a fist and a growl. He punched the spirit, sending it crashing through the trees. "You leave here. Now. I'll hold them off."

"Don't," Max said. "We barely got you away from the last one of these bastards."

"I learned a thing or two from that." Another purple sphere rose above one of the ghosts. Drummond adjusted his hat and narrowed his eyes at the spirit. "I can only buy you a little time. These things are just waking up. I can handle them. But once they get stronger, I'll jump into the Other. Meet up with you back at the house."

"But —"

"Don't argue. Get going."

J tugged on Max's hand as Drummond charged after another glob of purple energy. Ruby stood in the middle of it all, gazing upward with academic interest like an astronomy student on an outing. Madame Ti, however, watched events with ecstatic joy.

Max turned away, stumbling over rocks as Sandra and J led him toward the railroad tracks. When he realized where they headed, he yanked back. "Not that way. It's too far, too straight. They'll chase us down."

"Then what?" Sandra said, the fear rising in her voice.

He couldn't think of an answer. The idea that four inhuman spirits had been summoned stumped his mind. Four? They were supposed to be extremely rare, extremely dangerous — so much that many witches thought they were a myth — yet Madame Ti had used J's problem to summon four of them. She and Ruby had come all the way out here, crossing the lake and —

"The boat." Max shifted direction toward the water. "We'll use the boat they came in on."

Picking up speed, they dashed over the rocks and weeds. Purple light flashed like a growing storm, but Max kept his focus forward. He tightened his grip on J and tried to project all his love for this family.

"Think positive, good thoughts," he said. "These spirits thrive on negative feelings."

J said, "Kind of hard when we're running for our lives."

"I never said this job would be easy."

Though the jokes fell flat, Max warmed that J had not become a gibbering mess under all this pressure. Sandra pointed off to the left. "Over there. I see it."

The little motorboat had drifted off the ratty dock and caught up on some overgrowth. Max glanced back to see Drummond locking his arm around Miller while the three other purple ghosts moved in.

"He won't be able to hold out. Come on. Into the boat."

Max managed three strides toward the water when one of the inhuman spirits tore away from Drummond and blasted towards the boat. Not towards Max, Sandra, or J. The boat. With a horrid cry like a pig being slaughtered, the purple sphere smashed across the small craft, cutting it in half. As the two pieces took on water, the spirit rushed back and ripped across the outboard motor. Fire and sparks lit up the dark for less than a second. As the roar of destruction became a distant echo, as the flash of heat cooled with the night, the remains of the boat sank.

Stunned still, Max watched the bubbling waters swallow the boat. The purple sphere rushed back toward Drummond. It didn't even consider Max, Sandra, and J as a threat.

J splashed into the water up to his knees. He looked back at Max. "Come on. Don't stop."

"The boat's gone."

"But those aren't." He pointed to the life vests floating on the surface.

They were moving out of reach fast, but J wasn't grabbing them. He stood there frozen. Not with the same fear hitting them all. It never occurred to Max before, but J didn't know how to swim.

Max waded into the water — cold water, very cold. He hissed as he went deeper. He reached the first life vest with ease and tossed it back to J. The other two he would have to swim for.

In the distance, he could hear Madame Ti like a tent revival preacher. "Here before us is truly great power. Witchcraft is barely the start of what forces exist, and this inhuman spirit exemplifies a greater entity, a power beyond our mortal plane."

Paddling his way through the dark waters, Max's hand slapped upon the next vest. He stuck his head through one of the holes — maybe an arm hole, he didn't care — and he continued on for the third one.

"Do you see it, Ruby? Do you see how these marvels of raw energy do not fear us? They are not like ghosts — hiding, lonely, fearful. They are not like witches — clinging to each other, seeking strength in numbers. These are the binding forces of all existence, and now I've gained the knowledge and the power. They are mine to control."

Max grabbed the last vest and headed back. His teeth

chattered and his breath came out in staccato shivers. When he reached land, he handed Sandra a vest and readjusted the one ringing his head. "W-We have to swim out. Stay close. H-Hold onto each other. As long as we have faith in our family, in being together, we'll be protected. At least for long enough."

J said, "Miller won't come after us, and the others will stick by him cause they're all connected."

"How do you know that? Are you still tethered to Miller?"

"No, but before the spell broke him away, I had this feeling, like I knew all sorts of things about him. I can tell you that he hates that lake and will never go back to it. He just wants to rest. And since those purple things are now attached to him, and they're all connected to each other, I don't think any of them can get too far across the water."

As Sandra checked over J's life vest, Max snatched a glance at the graveyard. Drummond continued to punch, kick, and weave, but the spirits were clearly getting stronger. No more time left.

"Hurry," Max said, taking J's hand and leading the way into the icy lake. "This is going to be really cold."

Swimming out, Max watched as Drummond vanished into the Other.

Madame Ti laughed. "Flee like rats. It doesn't matter. I can harness these spirits. The power that the Brotherhood of the Rising sought is going to be mine. Cecily Hull thinks she can restore her family, but I'm the real force to control magic. Grandma Mobley? Mother Hope? They were but amateurs in my wake."

The further in the lake they swam, the less they could hear Madame Ti rambling on like a midnight drunk. Soon, all Max heard was the shivering breaths of his family and the shush of water as they paddled out.

"W-We'll be o-okay," he said. "A little m-more, and we'll cut back in to the r-railroad tracks. Sh-Should be far enough away from the s-spirits."

Swimming onward, Max chanced one final look back. The purple glow amongst the trees grew brighter, deeper in color, stronger. If there had only been one — only Miller — then maybe Sandra could have tackled opening another rift to remove the thing like she had the last time. But there were four. Four.

Tears welled in his eyes, but the lake water splashed them away.

Chapter 18

A DAMN INHUMAN SPIRIT. Max's foot pressed hard on the accelerator. The same kind of vicious specter that once altered his mind and nearly pushed him to Lizzie Borden his family. He swerved around a pothole, sweat stinging his eyes, as he barreled along the backroads. That horrible entity should never have been brought into the world. He shivered as his wet, cold clothes stuck to his skin.

"Honey," Sandra said. "Pull over. Let me drive."

"We can't stop. Not until we put serious distance between us and those things."

He alternated between the gas and the brake in order to negotiate an S-curve. The tires squealed their displeasure.

"Max, please."

"No, no. Those things are not getting into me again. And I refuse to let them have a try at you or J or PB."

In a soothing tone, Sandra said, "I know."

"You know? You're talking to me like I'm crazy. And what about Drummond? You think he wants to go through all that another time? That — that would be crazy."

"I think you are rightfully upset."

"Of course, I am. Why aren't you? Don't you see it now? This is why I didn't want J involved. This isn't a game. These spirits will destroy us. They'll destroy J and PB and everything we know and love."

"We beat one of them before."

"Barely." He blasted through an intersection and noticed Sandra's hand seizing the armrest. "I always knew it in the back of my mind, always knew that someday we'd come up against something beyond what we could handle."

"We don't know what we're up against."

"Four damn inhuman spirits. That's four too many."

"Hon, slow down. You're not thinking straight."

"Not thinking was agreeing to bring J to a place called Graveyard Island. Heck, the state would be smart to take the boys away from us. What kind of guardians are we?"

"I think you need to look in the rearview mirror."

"What? Are we being followed?" Max checked the mirror. Not a car in sight. But he caught a glimpse of J — wide-eyed alarm. Not from the ghosts, though. "Oh." Backing off the gas, Max slowed until he could safely pull onto the shoulder. Pushing back against the headrest, he let out a shaking breath.

"You okay?" Sandra asked.

Max shifted to look back at J. "Sorry about that."

Now that they weren't careening down a darkened road, J already appeared better. "No problem. You got scared. I'm guessing that happens now and then when dealing with ghosts and all this witchcraft stuff."

"It does." Max wiped the sweat from his brow. "But not usually like this."

Sandra stroked his cheek. "I'll drive the rest of the way. You relax. Panicking doesn't help, but being scared is not irrational." To J, she added, "We faced only one spirit that night we were at Reynolda House, and it's the reason our office burned down. It can get in your head and mess with your thoughts. It's very dangerous. So, don't hide anything strange that you experience. Okay?"

J nodded. "I'm sorry. I didn't know Miller was going to bring all this onto us."

"It's not your fault. Don't ever think it is."

"But if I hadn't started talking to Miller —"

"No," Max said. "Miller targeted you. And Madame Ti used us to summon these spirits. I don't know how she did it — this is very difficult magic — but she's clearly been trying to do this for a while."

Sandra said, "You're right. She knew what books to bring and the exacting nature of her spell. The Brotherhood needed older spells, non-witchcraft spells, and blood sacrifices to summon one spirit, but she's figured out how to do it with a casting circle and witchcraft. I should've seen it. All that precision she demanded, using all of us in the circle — those two points alone screamed that this was more than a tough location spell."

"What's the Brotherhood?" J asked.

As Max explained the nature of this ancient yet newly revitalized group of power-hungry fools, his pulse dropped and the tightness in his chest loosened. Sandra walked around the car and got in on the driver's side. Max slid over. She carefully pulled onto the road and headed home at a sensible speed.

When Max finished, J said, "Sounds like we can't really get away from these things if Madame Ti doesn't want us to. Right? I mean, when we swam off, she wasn't in any danger from them. Doesn't that kind of mean she's controlling them? Or at least has some deal with them?"

"Afraid so," Sandra said.

"Then we have to stop her, right?"

Max snorted a laugh. "Not so easy."

"We can't do what worked before," Sandra said. "Casting that spell wrecked me, could've killed me, but that's not the real reason."

"It's reason enough for me."

"I love you, too, honey. But the spell I used on that case had been designed to battle a spirit summoned by non-witchcraft. This is bound to be something quite different."

That surprised Max. He had been thinking they would simply find a way to amplify the original spell while also making it safer to use. But now ...

J said, "Tell me what to do. How can I help?"

"Not this time," Max said. "You've done a great job so far, but you're no longer connected to Miller. You don't have to be a part of this, and it's too dangerous."

"Stop that crap," J said, jutting his chin. "I've worked on plenty of cases with you guys. Maybe never this much, but I've seen the kinds of stuff you get messed up with. I've gone to the library and done research with Max, and I've sat in a casting circle and formed spells with Sandra. Uncle Drummond's taught me all about the Other and he's told me about all sorts of his old cases — things with mobsters and dead girls and curses that make you forget who you are and even spirits. Not inhuman ones, but one called an essence. I ain't a kid and I ain't stupid about all of this. So, shut up with the protective parent crap and tell me how I can help."

Max wondered if his mother had felt the same way when he first talked back to her. Worse than a slap in the face, Max felt mugged by the words. Yet he had a weird sense of pride that J had the strength to stand up for himself. Above it all, Max experienced a familiar sensation — one handed to him routinely by Sandra and summed up with a simple thought. J was right.

Max looked ahead at the road coming out of the darkness. "Last time we faced down an inhuman spirit, we had to stop it before dawn or it would grow too powerful to ever stop. These inhuman spirits from Graveyard Island did not behave like the one we fought before, and we've seen them tethered to each other, but we have to assume that a lot of the same rules apply. They feed off negative energy, we need to learn their names for whatever spell we use against them, and we have to rely on our faith in each other to protect us. Beyond that, I'm not sure where to start. We know so little. What we really need is a better idea of what we're dealing with."

Sandra said, "Then we should call in an expert."

"Yeah. I thought about her. I hate to disturb her after last time, but I don't see any other way. When we get back, I'll have Drummond contact her."

"Who?" J said. "What kind of expert?"

"She's a psychic, a real one, and she was integral to our success against the inhuman spirit last time. Her name's Irene Beck."

Chapter 19

DRY CLOTHES. Warm house. Hot coffee. In that order. Max, Sandra, and J indulged in the simple luxuries of life, permitting each bit of normalcy to restore them physically and mentally. Graveyard Island, Madame Ti, Ruby, the inhuman spirits — all melted away into the rich aroma of fresh-brewed caffeine.

When they first arrived home, they found Drummond waiting and anxious. "I know you had swimming to do, but did you have to joyride on the way back?"

Max laid out all that had happened and the conclusions they had made. Once he reached the main point — that they needed Irene Beck — Drummond left to fetch her. Max could have phoned the psychic, but she had a special bond with Drummond and considering that the clock read 1:37am, Max thought she might be more receptive if woken by a dear friend rather than a work-related acquaintance who tended to put her in life-threatening situations. Time was a factor, of course, but waiting an extra ten minutes for a more beneficial visit would save them more in the long run.

As they waited for Drummond and Irene to return, the Porters curled up in the living room — Sandra on one end of the couch, J on the other, and Max taking one of the reading chairs. Max and Sandra worked at their laptops while J hunched over his phone. Other than the occasional sip of coffee and the clack of keyboards, they stayed silent.

Until Sandra asked, "Do we need to talk?"

Though the question had been clearly directed toward J, the sentiment touched Max, too. He paused a moment to consider an answer. But before he could formulate the words, J covered them all. "I'm all talked out," the young man said.

Max returned to his laptop. The photos he had taken on Graveyard Island were all copied to the Cloud. Thankfully. His phone sat on the bedroom nightstand — back cover opened, lake water drained, and innards drying out. He didn't hold out much hope that the device could be salvaged, but he would try. In the meantime, he downloaded image after image and sipped coffee during the process.

The pictures of the various gravesites had come out clear. Part of him wondered if there would be blurry or strange formations — ghosts caught on camera. But he saw nothing so dramatic. Still, he had solid shots of Miller's grave, and that alone might provide them with crucial information.

Or perhaps not. Perhaps he was spinning his wheels while watching the clock count down.

He did have about ten pictures of the two casting circles Madame Ti had used for the spells. Those he sent over to Sandra, and she got working on them right away.

"A lot of the symbols we used on these spells were new to me," Sandra said as she tried to connect the pictures with her memory, then with her favored online witchcraft resources. "A few of them looked like combinations of older, basic symbols every witch uses, but I think that Madame Ti may have been building her own."

J perked up. "Custom symbols? I didn't know you could do that."

"Making them is easy. Even I can make a new symbol by bastardizing a few old ones. But making ones that actually harness power, that actually work — that's high-level stuff. In fact, I can't think of single witch we've known that ever did it."

"That's just great," Max said, rubbing his eyes with his palms. "Madame Ti is turning out to be far worse than we realized. I wonder if Cecily Hull has any idea the Pandora's Box she's opened by teaming with this woman."

Headlights flashed along the walls as Irene Beck pulled into the driveway. Max opened the side door and welcomed her through the kitchen. When she entered the living room still wearing a nightgown and wrapped in a housecoat, Irene's focus turned straight to J.

"Why hello there," she said, her thick North Carolina accent filling the room as much as her presence. Max always marveled that such a small lady commanded such a powerful stature.

Adjusting her glasses, she scooted onto the couch — her feet clad in fuzzy slippers dangled over the edge — and offered her hand to J. "Do you remember me? I once drove you and your brother off the road. Well, more precisely, you boys were being kidnapped, and I drove the perpetrators off the road."

J shook her hand. "I remember, ma'am."

"Good manners. I like that."

Drummond appeared in the doorway. "I told you he's a great kid. I've been teaching him how to be a proper gentleman."

This was news to Max, but before he could press Drummond on the subject, Irene said, "Seems like y'all are doing a wonderful job raising young J here. But J, you know you're already smart and full of strength, don't you? Why I recall how brave you were that night I helped you, and from what your Uncle Drummond tells me, you were equally brave this night. You are to be commended."

"Thanks. I don't think I was so brave, though. More scared than anything."

"Bravery is all about doing what needs doing despite being scared. You think your pal, Drummond, never gets scared?"

"He's a ghost. He does the scaring."

Irene tittered. "Oh, you are a pickle. Better watch this one, Sandra. He's going to have the ladies lining up for a block-and-a-half."

Sandra said, "He's already starting to date."

"Is he now? Well, Mr. J, you may not know this, but I run a small shop specializing in materials of the occult and witchcraft. You come visit me sometime, and I'll see that you receive a special gift." Pushing off the couch, Irene went on, "But for now, we have to discuss more pressing matters. Ain't that right, Max?"

Gesturing with his mug, Max said, "You want coffee, there's a mostly fresh pot in the kitchen. Otherwise, yeah, we need to get talking."

With a firm tug on her belt, she said, "My dear Drummond was kind enough to fill me in on the basic situation. Seems you've had yourselves another encounter with an inhuman spirit."

Sandra said, "Four, actually."

"Four? Do tell."

She spent the next several minutes detailing all that had happened from the moment J introduced them to Private Miller. As Sandra spoke, as the picture became clearer, lines furrowed along Irene's forehead and her mouth shrank to a small dot. When Sandra finished, Irene asked to look over the pictures.

"Well?" Max finally said. "How do we handle four inhuman spirits?"

"I have no idea." She stepped into the center of the room. "Lucky for you, this is only one."

"No, we distinctly saw four."

"You saw four spheres of energy all tied together by tethers of energy, correct?"

Sandra nodded. "You're saying they're all one being split into four?"

"Exactly. One inhuman spirit ripped apart into four unique pieces. And as I understand it, you already know the name of this spirit."

"Wardarit. Madame Ti called it by name several times."

Drummond said, "If there's only one and we know its name, can't we perform the same spell as last time?"

"No, dear. That spell was designed not only to banish the spirit away from our plane of existence, but more importantly, we used that spell to call you back. Thankfully, you're right here. Quite safe. But even if we could tailor that old spell, it would not work. You see, an inhuman spirit gives itself away by its behavior. At Reynolda House, y'all experienced a spirit that reveled in your anguish. One that attacked you repeatedly. One that explicitly told you it sought a body and a soul to possess. From what you've said, none of those things apply to Wardarit."

Sandra said, "It never tried to possess us, but it did destroy the boat. It tried to stop us from leaving."

"Yet it did not pursue you."

"Because of Madame Ti. She controls it."

With a disappointed sigh, Irene said, "Have you not learned yet? Nobody truly controls an inhuman spirit."

Max said, "If Wardarit isn't trying to possess us, then it's not trying to live in our world."

"Now you're thinking again. I believe you are absolutely correct."

"Then what does it want?"

"My best guess — it wants to go home. And all y'all need to help it."

Max narrowed his eyes at Irene as if she had suddenly become blurry. "You want us to help a psychotic ball of energy that, for the moment, wants to go home but could easily change its mind and slaughter all of us in seconds — is that right? We'll need to drive several hours back to Graveyard Island, assuming it's still there, figure out exactly what's going on with it, what kind of spell brought it here, design a new spell to send it back where it came from, risk our lives performing the spell, and all the time, avoid Madame Ti and Ruby from stopping us. Oh, and we'll have to do it before morning, which is about four hours away, or things will really turn ugly."

"You're certainly in a mood tonight." Settling next to J once again, she said, "Don't worry, it's not all as bad as you say. From what Sandra and Drummond have told me, it is quite clear that time is not a factor to be concerned with. That spirit has been split apart and attached to four very old ghosts. If it were like the other one, if it sought freedom in our world, then you would have known it by now. Seems to me that this spirit is caged, in a manner of speaking — locked into these ghosts and summoned by a witch who hopes to gain control of them for their power."

"Then we still have to worry about Madame Ti."

"You should always worry about her. In this case, she is more dangerous than usual. Right now, she's probably straining to assert her dominance over the spirit. She's like a lion tamer, and she's got one seriously pissed off lion."

With a startling clap, Drummond said, "Sounds like we need to get the spirit on its way home before Madame Ti takes control of it. How do we do that?"

"Something is keeping it attached to those ghosts. That's the cage it finds itself within."

"Madame Ti's spell?" J asked.

"She's strong, but not that strong. After all, if she could summon and imprison an inhuman spirit whenever she wanted, she would already have done it. She'd have control of all the witches in all of the world."

Sandra said, "It was summoned here somehow, though."

"Probably the spell required an object to latch the spirit into this world."

"Something related to these ghosts."

"That is exactly right. You find that object and you destroy it, and with any luck, the spirit will be on its way. Much like I must be now."

"Hold on, doll," Drummond said, swishing in front of her. "We need you."

"I doubt that. I'm still not fully recovered from the first time we faced a spirit, and quite frankly, one time was enough. I like excitement in my life, but y'all are crazy as far as I'm concerned. Now, I'm happy to help you when I can, but I won't be facing off with an inhuman spirit anytime soon. Hopefully, never again."

Sandra said, "But I needed you to pull off that spell."

"And you have lived almost another year since then. Learned nearly a year's worth more of life. I suspect you'll be able to apply those lessons to your current predicament."

Max wanted to stand and shout and bully her into staying, but he remained seated. No good ever came from such behavior. "Thank you for coming out so late at night, and thank you for pointing us in the right direction."

"You're very welcome. I do understand the serious nature of these events, so if there is any way in which I can provide assistance that doesn't require my physical presence in front of the spirit, I will gladly help. I'm only a phone call away." She made sure to nod at each member of the team, finishing with J. "Good luck to you."

Adjusting her robe, she walked out of the house. Max only then noticed she still wore slippers.

"Well," Sandra said, "I guess we're on our own."

Chapter 20

NOBODY COULD SLEEP. Not only from the constant adrenaline jolts they had received all night, but also from downing several pots of coffee. On top of it all, Irene Beck had backed out of any further involvement, leaving the heavy lifting to the Porter Agency. Max couldn't blame her — she had already been more involved in their cases than she ever wanted — but he hated her timing.

"I guess we're back to the starting line on this one," he said, after Irene's car drove away.

"Not exactly." Sandra stood by the front door and observed the late-night street. "We know a lot more than we did before, and that means we won't be throwing darts in the dark."

"Very true. But we still have to rebuild the groundwork."

After a short discussion, they decided that Sandra would use the photos of Madame Ti's casting circle to research what kind of spell had been created. Even if Madame Ti had concocted the whole thing on her own, it had to be based on other spells. From those, Sandra might be able to discern how parts of the newer spell operated. Max, on the other hand, had more direct research to do. Since this spirit had been locked into four specific ghosts, he wanted to know all he could find on them. It wouldn't be easy, but if the other soldiers had a connection to Miller, there would be a chance. As for J, they gave him the choice. He picked Sandra.

Max tried not to feel jealous, and for the most part, he succeeded. It had been a long night, and he had behaved poorly. If given the choice, he would have picked Sandra, too.

Left on his own, he gathered his things and headed out to the Z. Smith Reynolds Library. Of course, the place was closed at

2:45am, but he needed a change of scenery to concentrate, and by the time the library did open, he wanted to be first to get in. While he believed Irene when she said they weren't under a time constraint, he also had enough encounters with the paranormal world to make him wary. Besides, even if the spirit was in no hurry, they lacked the same assurances regarding Madame Ti.

The faster they resolved this case, the better.

He parked in the biology department lot at Wake Forest University. The library sat a short walk away, and he didn't expect many students to be bothering him early on a Sunday morning. As long as campus security left him alone, he could work in the car, catch a little sleep, and be ready to follow up any queries once he got inside the building.

With a roll of his neck and a quick crack of the knuckles, he launched into Private Miller's life. Digging around census information and school records, he tried to locate anything that would be useful. After a half hour, he realized his mistake — probably would have picked up on it sooner, but his brain had been through a lot of turmoil that night — and he redirected his efforts to surround the years in the Confederacy. After all, that was the time he would have had the most contact with these other soldiers.

Since they were all buried in the small towns flooded for Badin Lake, and their bodies were all relocated to Graveyard Island, Max returned to the Civil War registry to cross reference soldiers from those towns who also served with Miller. He managed to whittle down the possible names to eleven young men.

Max halted his work as instinct sent warnings through his body. He craned around the seat to view through each of the car windows. Nothing. Nobody. Wanting to dismiss the feeling, he turned back to his research, but that itch on his neck kept saying that somebody watched him.

With a shiver, he resumed working on the list of names. One by one, he delved into them and soon discarded four. Two died right after the war ended — one in California and the other in Texas. A third lived in Whitney for at least a decade but died on a fishing boat and his body was never recovered. The fourth man died during the construction of the dam that would create Badin Lake and therefore never was buried in a grave that required being moved. That left seven names. Four too many.

Another idea struck Max, and after several searches, he discovered Miller's nuptial announcement in the archives of the *Watchman and Old North State* — an area newspaper than ran from 1830 - 1929. *The Heron family of Whitney is pleased to announce the engagement of their daughter, Maybelle Rose, to the gentleman, Private Alexander Miller, also of Whitney this June, 1868.* In the article, two of the names from Max's list were mentioned — Brody Denver and Michael Shoemaker. Brody was to be Miller's best man and Michael would serve in the wedding party. Which left Max with five names and one open spot. He suspected that when he dug into the lives of Miller's friends, he had a good chance of stumbling upon one of the names in his final list. He hoped.

"Good morning, partner," Drummond said, lowering through the car roof.

"Not morning yet. Sun's got a bit of waiting to do." Max saved his work and closed the laptop. He knew the old ghost well enough — Drummond planned to talk. "What did you want?"

"Thought I'd check in. See how everybody is doing."

"I'm fine. Just trying to work in peace. You should check on Sandra and J. They rattle more than I do."

Drummond raised his eyebrows as he lowered his head. "Do I really need to point out the fallacy of that statement?"

"Okay. Maybe I've been more rattled this time."

"*This time?* When hasn't Sandra been the rock of your relationship?"

Max sliced his hand through the air, accidently nicking part of Drummond and feeling the numb chill rush up his fingers. "Did you come here with information or are you simply trying to annoy me? You're doing great at the latter, by the way."

"This case has really wound you up."

"No kidding. What baffles me is how calm you are about it all. I get that on other cases, the threat to you is minimal. Your concern usually is for the safety of Sandra, the Sandwich Boys, or even me. But this — last time we faced an inhuman spirit, you nearly were lost forever. How can you not be *wound up* over facing another one?"

Crossing his arms, Drummond looked ahead as if they were driving instead of sitting in a parking lot. "Don't mistake my being calm for not being concerned. I take this case very seriously. Maybe more than any case we've ever had because this time J is directly involved. And I like that kid."

"That's exactly it. Without J being involved, I'd still be uptight — the threat to all of us, including you, is too high with these spirits — but at least I know that we've defeated one before. Even then, people died. If J comes to harm because of this —"

"It won't be your fault. You forget, J has the touch, the gift, the whatever-you-want-to-call-it. He can see ghosts. Without you and Sandra, he'd be stuck trying to figure out all that on his own. If you had never come into the boys' lives, they would have found a way to survive and maybe even thrive. J's very smart. He could've done it. And he still has to. Yeah, you gave him a roof and some stability, but like everybody in this world, J has to stand on his own at some point. I think he's taking a few of those *tentative* steps right now."

Reclining his seat back a little, Max massaged his stiff neck. "It certainly seems that way, though I wouldn't call him tentative. Dating and wanting to help a ghost and now wanting to work a case in-depth — he's not shy about jumping into the deep end."

Drummond chuckled. "I guess not."

Max joined in. "Not at all."

Both men paused for a breath. Then they broke out into hearty laughter. It only lasted a few seconds, but it flushed Max's body and relaxed his muscles.

Opening his laptop, he said, "I've found names on two of Miller's three ghost pals. I'd say you should go to the Other and see if you can find them, but I doubt they can leave this world any more than Miller can. And now that they're all locked down with this spirit, I doubt they can leave Graveyard Island at all."

Drummond listened as he tapped his chin. "That's it?"

"I've plucked out two names from over a century ago with

nothing to go on but that they were in the same army as Miller. That isn't enough?"

"Don't get huffy. I only meant that I don't hear anything about witchcraft. No mention of the Brotherhood of the Rising. How are these men all caught up with an inhuman spirit? What stupid thing did they do that traces all the way to today?"

"I have no idea. It doesn't make any sense. You think about all the witches we've dealt with — they aren't very subtle. Not once you know about them, about what to look for. When you know the signs to read, you can see witchcraft everywhere it's been used. But these guys — nothing."

"You forget, though, that when I tried to find out about Miller in the Other, every ghost clammed up. Even if Miller's friends are just average joes, Miller's something else."

"You think he's the ringleader? Maybe he tried to summon an inhuman spirit and it all went wrong?"

"Maybe, but I doubt it. Not unless you find some nugget that indicates he, at the very least, dabbled in witchcraft at one point."

Gesturing to the laptop screen, Max said, "You can see what I got. Maybe somebody in his family was involved in casting spells, but if so, I don't think he knew about it. He certainly didn't get his hands dirty enough to leave a trace."

"Family?" Drummond perked up, floating over the seat. "Pal, you've given me a good idea. You get some rest. I'm going back to the Other."

Before Max could ask a single question, Drummond vanished. The car became extra quiet and a bit warmer. Max fished out his phone and texted Sandra with an update. Sandra responded that she and J were doing fine, although they were both frustrated. Each time they thought they had unraveled Madame Ti's symbols to reveal the core components, they would arrive at results that made no sense or were flat-out wrong. But J's good attitude kept them at it.

Max set his head back and closed his eyes. He went over the case step by step — he tried to, anyway. Somewhere along the process, he fell asleep.

* * * *

Two things woke Max — the sunrise and Drummond. Startling at the old ghost's loud call of *Wake up, partner!* Max bumped his knee into the steering wheel. He looked around, confused for a few seconds, and tried to work out the knot in the back of his neck.

"You're going to be happy about this," Drummond said.

"Whatever you're going to say, does it come with coffee and a bagel?"

"Not at all. But it does come with you needing to spark yourself awake. We've got an interview to conduct."

"Interview?"

"What you said last night — er, a few hours ago — about Miller's family and his problems tracing all the way to today ... well, I went into the Other and decided to do some genealogical legwork." Drummond tipped back his hat and kicked up his feet — which floated through the windshield but didn't stop him from grinning. "See, I figured that just because I couldn't get anybody to talk to me directly about Miller didn't meant I couldn't get them to talk to me indirectly. This is a good detective lesson for you to learn — people love to talk. Always. These ghosts were scared to say anything until I gave them a loophole that allowed them to share what they knew."

"What loophole?"

"Family. The ghosts from the Civil War that most likely knew of Miller or heard of him, the ones the most afraid to talk to me about Miller, they were more than happy to open up about Miller's family. In particular, they told me that he had two kids — a boy and a girl. Another ghost listening in was eager to share that the girl was still in the Other. Only took a few hours of hoofing it around until I'd worked my way up to Sid Carter."

"And he is?"

"Miller's great-great-great-grandson. More importantly, he's alive and living in Burlington. I even got an address for you. Should be able to get there in about two hours."

Max started the car. "If I could pat you on the back, I would."

"I appreciate the sentiment."

Chapter 21

DRIVING TO BURLINGTON meant a long stretch on 40 East with nothing to do but think. Normally, Max would relish the opportunity — on a case, he would reevaluate every aspect of events; off a case, he would ponder Sandra, the boys, his life or simply let his thoughts wander wherever they wanted to go. This time, however, he worried.

"Last case really hit you hard," Drummond said from the passenger seat.

"I'm fine."

"Even if I hadn't been a detective for over eighty years, I certainly know you well enough by now. You are not fine."

"I'm just worried about J."

"It's more than that. I've seen you losing your head over the Sandwich Boys before, and this ain't that. It's the inhuman spirit."

"What the hell else would it be?" Max spit the words with a fury he had not realized welled within his chest. Now that the heat had been unleashed, it raged across his body. "I'm so sick of these witches and cultists and power-hungry families all trying to steal some advantage in life by using magic. What is wrong with people? How many times do they have to almost die or lose a loved one or see somebody's entire future corrupted and destroyed? How many times before they stop and think *Huh? Maybe messing with witchcraft isn't such a great idea* and leave it all behind?"

"Since witchcraft goes back well over a thousand years, I'm not holding my breath for a sudden epiphany on their part — even if I had breath to hold."

Having spewed out his frustration, Max already cooled a bit.

"Mostly, I wish I knew how to change J's mind. Redirect him into something that might give him a pleasant life. It's too late for Sandra and me — even if we wanted out of it all, the Hulls and the covens and the Brotherhoods will never let us go."

"Ah, I see now."

"What's there to suddenly see? I think I'm being quite clear about it all."

"You're also avoiding the big part — the reason you're feeling this way now. And it ain't J. Not exactly."

Max saw exit signs for Burlington, glanced at his phone displaying the GPS map and route to Sid Carter's home, and eased over a lane to take the next off ramp. "If you got a point to make, you better make it quick. We'll be there in a few minutes, and I could use a little time to prepare."

"No point to make. Just an observation. Last case, we went up against Oxorot — an inhuman spirit that ripped through us with ease. Really took a beating before we prevailed. Even then, we had our lumps, more than any other case I can think of. Irene had told us these inhuman spirits were very rare, yet here we are again with another one. It's like you said — our enemies keep messing around with these things they barely know how to handle. Might as well be a toddler playing with a loaded pistol. Thing is — if they're a bunch of children in danger, that makes us the protectors, right? I think you're all upset because it's finally hitting you."

"What? That we have to be the parents to these stupid children?"

"No. That we have to take the loaded pistol out of their hands. And that means we end up holding it. If we're not careful, we end up getting shot."

Max gave his head a vigorous shake. "I think I've lost the thread of this metaphor."

"Look, it's like this — you're finally accepting that in order to keep all these witches and such in line, we have to accept the risks of what they do. This case, for example. None of us — including J — would ever have to deal with an inhuman spirit if not for Madame Ti bringing it about. Or the previous case with the Brotherhood."

"And?"

"I think part of you had managed to lie to yourself after the last case. Told yourself that the spirit, Oxorot, was a one-time thing, and you'd never have to deal with anything like that again. Just spend the rest of your life fighting good ol' ghosts and curses like you had become accustomed to."

Max took the exit and quickly drove out of the built-up sections of Burlington. A few sleepy developments slid by and then they hit the rural area. Homes and fields were separated by patches of woods. The occasional gas station or convenience store popped up. Not many people on the road — it was Sunday morning, after all — and the gray sky blanketing the area combined with Drummond's words to ease Max more. Sometimes hearing one's fears stated made them less frightening.

"With this new spirit, Wardarit, I can't pretend anymore."

"Afraid not. And that fact grates against your hopes for J."

"Because he's diving headfirst into all of this, and I can't stop him."

Drummond motioned as if tossing the thoughts out the window. "Just my observations. But like you said, we're almost at Carter's house. We need to get focused."

With a bitter chuckle, Max said, "As if you weren't doing that this entire time. Getting me out of my head so I can see the case for what it is."

"Don't know about any of that. But I do know that my partner is at his best when he can push aside his fear and stay clear-headed on the moment."

Taking a deep breath, Max checked the GPS again, made a turn onto a side road and tried hard to be Drummond's best partner.

The further they traveled down the road, the worse conditions became. Macadam turned into loose gravel turned into dirt. The sidewalks disappeared becoming drainage ditches and then finally nothing but weeds encroaching across the road — *dusty path* was more accurate. Even the houses went from full-sized houses to starter homes to spacious but falling apart buildings that probably would have been condemned, if anybody from the government bothered to drive out this far.

Sid Carter lived in an old farmhouse with a wraparound porch. Max guessed that much of the surrounding land had once been the farm, but over the decades, pieces were sold away until finally all that remained was the original house and a small plot with three large oak trees. The house next door had a tall chain-link fence and a vicious dog that snarled and barked at Max's car as he parked. So much for a quiet approach. In fact, by the time Max left the car and walked up to the porch, Sid Carter leaned on a support post and tapped out a cigarette.

He was a tall man. Skinny with sallow eyes and ragged salt-and-pepper hair. He smelled like an ashtray and looked no better. "Can I help you?" he asked, lighting up and flicking the match off into the overgrowth between houses.

"Hi, there. I'm Max Porter. I'm from Wake Forest University."

This wasn't the first time Max had pretended to be somebody else nor was it the first time he felt the sharp scrutiny of the person he sought to deceive. He knew the unspoken rules. Max halted about halfway to the porch — close enough to talk but far enough back to be non-threatening.

"University boy, huh?" Carter said, smoke puffing out as he spoke.

"That's right, sir. Though at my age, I don't think *boy* is the proper term." Max forced a chuckle and was pleased to see Carter snicker.

Drummond continued forward, slipping through the walls of the house. He would inspect the entire building, and Max offered a little thought of thanks to have a ghost for a partner. It certainly came with advantages.

"Well, Mr. Porter, what is it that I can do for you?"

"I'm researching descendants from the Civil War, and I was hoping you'd spare a little time to chat."

With a slow nod, as if each word needed to be digested

carefully, Carter took a long drag to finish his cigarette. Like the match, he flicked the stub into the grass and headed toward the front door. "Come on in."

Max approached at a leisurely pace, waiting for Drummond to let him know if it was safe to enter. Apparently, he moved too slow this time. Carter came back out and motioned into the house.

"I'm coming," Max said. "My legs are a bit stiff from the driving."

"More likely from spending too much time behind a desk. You want a beer?"

"That would be appreciated." Max had no interest in a beer, but hospitality had its rules. Especially when trying to pry information from a person.

Drummond poked his head out of a closed window. "All good in here. Nobody else home and no signs of witchcraft. But he packs the place like a witch."

Max entered the house and grinned. While Carter did appear to be a packrat, it was not in a witchy way. Witches often hoarded everything they could get their hands on. But Carter had a specific interest in what he filled his house with — books. Stacks and stacks of hardbacks and paperbacks. Carter was a bookworm.

Walking over from the kitchen, his boots clumping on the warped wood floor, Carter said, "I can see your surprise. Don't worry. Most people around here are surprised first time they come in."

As Max sauntered further in, he checked the spines and covers of various books — *Flint* by Louis L'Amour, *Beloved* by Toni Morrison, *The Caves of Steel* by Isaac Asimov, *The Brothers Karamazov* by Dostoevsky, *Off Season* by Jack Ketchum, as well as copies of the Tao Te Ching, the Bhagavata, and the Holy Bible. No books on witchcraft. Not even a history of the practice.

"You certainly have eclectic taste," Max said.

Carter sat on a metal folding chair by a card table and indicated another folding chair. He set two cans of beer on the table and popped them both open. "I'm a man who values a true education — one that never stops. It's been my experience that reading is one of the best educators around. Teaches you how to think as well as empathize. Frankly, half the crap this country suffers from and half the nonsense we fall prey to is because we don't read enough. Take you, for example."

"Me?"

"If I wasn't a well-read man, I might actually believe you're from Wake and fall prey to whatever crap and nonsense you want to shovel my way."

While Max never liked being pegged, it had happened before. He knew how to recover. And so did his partner. Without even a glance, Drummond flew off into the rest of the house to find any bit of information, any angle they could make use of. In the meantime, Max had to dig himself out of the hole he had fallen into.

Taking a sip of the beer, he flashed a bashful smile. "I am sorry, Mr. Carter. I meant no offense. I've learned the hard way that most folks don't want to hear the truth from me. It's easy to give them a story that fits into what they expect."

"Well, I think we've established that I am not like most folks."

"We certainly have."

"Now, unless you want me to go into my bedroom and bring out my 12-gauge, I suggest you start telling me some truth here. Who are you? And what do you really want?"

"Everything I said was true except the part about working for Wake. Lying is easier when it's mostly true, and throwing in a school like Wake or Duke usually stops people questioning any doubts in the back of their minds."

"Okay. I can accept that. But now, Mr. Porter, I got more questions. Who do you really work for, and why are you lying about researching Civil War descendants?"

Max took another sip of his beer that turned into a full gulp as he peeked from wall to wall. No Drummond. Just Sid Carter's strong face staring, waiting for an answer, and daring Max to fib once more.

"I work for myself," Max said, handing over a business card for The Porter Agency. "I'm a private researcher specializing in unusual and difficult to find information. The work that brings me here is not something I was hired to do. I'm actually trying to help out a young man, and his problems led to research that led me here."

"A problem involving my heritage?"

As Max tried to pull out a reasonable explanation that would still leave him opportunities to get what he needed, Drummond thankfully returned. "You can drop the act. He's got a glass case in his bedroom with all sorts of family war memorabilia. Hit him direct and you'll be fine."

Setting the beer can back on the table, Max stared straight at Carter. "My current case has involved locating the grave of a Confederate soldier, Private Alexander Miller. Turns out he's buried on Graveyard Island."

"Hell, I could've told you that all along. That's why you're here?"

"I'm trying to get more information on him, and I was able to trace his lineage down to you. The records on him are rather scant and incomplete."

Carter screwed up his mouth while drumming his fingers on his knee. "I think I got some bits you might be interested in. Come on with me."

They walked to a back bedroom, and as Drummond had reported, there was a glass case — a large cabinet, really — filled with objects covering Carter's family history. On one shelf, there were two purple hearts, a World War II helmet, a canteen from Vietnam, a name tag and the US flag arm patch. Another shelf held a bayonet, a British World War I field manual, and a crimp-edged photo of a sailor with a lovely Korean girl in Seoul. Two ancient service revolvers, some sort of whistle, and a few letters also graced this miniature museum. Stacks of books about various wars involving the United States guarded either side of the cabinet.

"At the top," Carter said.

Max checked out the highest shelf and found a framed photograph staring back at him — fifteen men in Confederate garb standing near a tent in the middle of the woods. Alexander

Miller's blurred face stood out two from the left end. And next to the soldier, despite the shoddy picture, Max knew he saw Brody Denver, Miller's best man.

Turning back to Carter, Max said, "Do you know when or where that photo was taken?"

"Middle of the war is my best guess because later he would've been at Salisbury."

"Salisbury? Was that a battle? I didn't think he saw much action."

Carter shifted some books off the side of his bed and plunked down. "Come on now, Mr. Porter, I thought we were done with the lying. You wouldn't be here talking with me if this wasn't about Salisbury."

Max's eyes darted to the corner where Drummond floated, but the ghost shrugged. "I'm sorry if I offended you, but I really don't know about Salisbury."

Bending forward to rest his elbows on his knees, Carter shook his head. "You think I'm that much of a fool. A stranger comes to my house, lies to me, then tells me he is a researcher of the odd and unusual, happens to be looking into old Private Miller, and yet he don't know about the curse of Salisbury?"

"A curse." Max tamped down the eagerness in his voice. "I didn't know about any curse, but you're right — that is exactly the kind of thing I came here hoping to learn. What happened in Salisbury?"

Carter reached under the bed and pulled out a book. He looked at the cover a moment before tossing it at Max's feet. "That'll give you the gory details."

As Max bent to pick up the book, he heard two things that froze his heart — Drummond calling his name and the distinct click of a 12-gauge shotgun's safety flicked off. Leaving the book alone, Max raised his hands. He had his trusty 9mm in his pocket, but even if he could manage the heroic speed required to get it out, it was still useless — he had yet to load the weapon.

"The fact is that Private Alexander Miller was a fine man, known locally for being charitable even when he had so little to his name," Carter said, making each word sound like a threat.

"The fact is that Private Alexander Miller never did wrong to nobody. He only fought in the war because he was drafted and refused to be locked away as an objector. Back then, prison life was worse than most things. But he never owned a slave and never thought much of those who did. In fact, according to my family history, Miller believed that God and Jesus would want all mankind to be equal, and so he treated all as such. It was his own misfortune to be born in a time and place where his views were frowned upon. There was never a finer man than Private Alexander Miller." Using the barrel to gesture at the door, he added, "I think you've overstayed your welcome."

Drummond hovered behind Carter. "Just say the word, and he'll have an icy headache he won't ever forget."

Max noticed Carter's finger sat on the trigger. This man was serious and irresponsible. Max made a slight motion with his head — *no.* If Drummond touched this man, that trigger finger might twitch, and Max would end up with a jagged hole punched through his torso.

"You think you're the first ever to ask about Salisbury? Been a long time, I'll admit, but others come before you. Mostly old women. Always wanting to know the ugliness of it all. I didn't like it then, and I don't like it now. All that superstitious crap — it drove my mama nutty. Everything that went wrong in her life, she blamed it on that curse. Same as her mama. Not me, though. I refuse to let a bunch of old wives' tales ruin me like that. But at least those women were family. At least they had a reason to believe it in all. It's you folks that make me sick. Gettin' off on other people's misery and misfortune. Disgusting."

"That's not what I'm doing. I want to help."

"Sure you do. Like all those fine folks who only wanted to write a book or make their documentary films or whatnot. Only trying to help yourself to some fame off my family's problems is more like it."

Max scooted toward the hallway. "Okay. You're right. I should never have come here. I apologize. I'm leaving now."

Drummond said, "Trust me. I got an idea."

Max wanted to scream at his partner, but he focused on

backing up without tripping over the various stacks of books. Drummond flew around front and grabbed the shotgun's barrel — not hard enough to cause the excruciating pain of direct contact with the corporeal world, but enough to chill the metal barrel. Colder and colder the temperature of the shotgun dropped as Max inched closer to the exit.

"What the hell?" Carter noticed the frosty white spreading from the end of his weapon. The man slipped his finger off the trigger. He held the shotgun sideways as if he could diagnose the trouble by looking at it. With a snarl on his lips, he said, "You better be gone by the time I fix this, or I'm calling you an ambulance."

Max knew better than to bother with any parting words. He rushed out of the house, got in his car, and hurried back toward the highway. When his phone rang, he let out a screech and ignored Drummond's laughter.

He pulled over, not trusting his shaking hands to manage driving and a phone. "Hello?" He forgot to even check who was calling.

"Hi, hon," Sandra said. "PB just called. He's ready to come back. You mind picking him up?"

Chapter 22

PB STOOD OUTSIDE Mrs. Porter's apartment building. That struck Max as odd. In the past, he would usually have to go knocking on his mother's door to get their attention. Or, at the least, send a text to PB's phone.

"Things go bad?" Max asked as they drove off.

PB appeared to weigh out his answer for a moment. "Just different."

"Try to remember that she's the one dealing with this disease all the time. We get to walk away from it. It may make her close off a bit."

"That's what I was expecting, but she opened up about everything."

"Oh." Max stayed quiet for a few blocks while he shoved back any iota of jealousy creeping through his bones.

"I think she wanted to prepare me for what would be coming in the next few years. Or months, if this turns out worse than she thinks."

"Are you okay?"

"Like you said, she's the one going through all this. I mean I'm sad, of course. But I don't have that magic view of things that little kids hold — y'know, that everything can be fixed and there's always a solution to making the world right the way you want it. Fact is that people get sick and die. Sometimes you can't change that. Most of the time, I guess."

For the rest of the drive, they did not speak. Max had told Sandra that he witnessed a new maturity in these boys, but what he saw now made his earlier claim naïve. PB had gone far beyond. He was a man, now. The way he held himself, the way he thought about others, the way he had started to understand the cruel side of life — all signs of adulthood. All hard lessons to learn. And how one handles that newfound knowledge often determined the quality of a person. Max smiled at how great PB's qualities had proven to be.

Perhaps the time had come to share the truth with PB. In the past, he had resisted the strange things he experienced, showing Max and Sandra that he could not accept the reality that they knew. But with Max's mother beginning her decline, perhaps knowing that ghosts exist and that Mrs. Porter might stick around for a while after her death — perhaps that would offer some comfort. Of course, even if Max opened that much of the door, he would not bring up the idea of witches, curses, or spirits. That would only shut PB's brain right back down.

They pulled into the driveway, and Max turned off the car. "You know, there are things about death that you probably should hear."

"Once, back when J and I lived on the streets, I saw a man die." PB looked right into Max. "About a block from where you would bring me food. It was late one night, later than I should've been out — not safe, y'know — and I was scavenging for whatever I could find. Don't know what made me think to go out that night, but I did. This drunk came wobbling up the sidewalk. Front of his pants were wet and he had puke on his shirt. Couple of guys showed up to roll him and I hid by a dumpster. Watched the whole thing. I don't think they meant to kill the guy, but they hit him hard. A lot. Kicked him and punched him and messed him up really bad. After they left, I snuck out, happy to have gone unnoticed, and then I saw the guy's eyes. That's when it happened. Something in them snapped out, went away, and I knew — he was gone."

"I'm sorry you had to see that."

"What I saw was somebody afraid. There was no peace in his death. Not even a willingness to accept it. That guy was staring out at the night, at me, and knowing he was about to die and all he had was regret and fear. But Grandma Porter isn't like that. She's already taking steps to be ready. She's trying to be brave about it all, and I think if I'm the same way, then maybe it'll make things easier on her."

Max gave PB a squeeze on the shoulder and kept his mouth shut. As strong as PB had proven to be, he didn't need a greater burden at the moment. Still, at some point, someday, Max knew he would have to tell PB everything. After all, he and Sandra were responsible for these young men. They were supposed to be the ones in charge so that—

Max stopped breathing as his mind fired off an idea. A strong one.

"You okay?" PB asked.

Taking in a sharp breath, Max grinned. "Something you said may have helped out our current case. Thanks."

"Um, sure. No problem."

Chapter 23

MUCH OF THE AFTERNOON ZIPPED BY in a haze of research. If pressed, Max could recall Sandra letting him know that she had some promising leads on the spell and wanted to find out more about the inhuman spirit. He grunted his agreement with the plan and muttered that he had an idea to follow up. She knew him too well after all the years and let him go. But not before mentioning that J had worked hard and wanted to take the afternoon off with his girlfriend, Janal. Max thought he agreed to that, too, but added that Drummond should chaperone — in case Ruby showed up again. As for PB, the young man thumped off to his room to sleep.

But all of that slipped through Max's attention as he grabbed his laptop, powered up at his kitchen cubicle, and got to work. His idea — when searching for information about a specific soldier in the military, especially in a wartime military, the best place to go would be up the chain of command. If anybody had recorded anything important about Miller, it would come from his immediate superiors — the ones required to report everything regarding those they were in charge of.

Max figured the best place to start his search for Miller's boss would be with where Miller had been stationed — Salisbury. Starting with a simple google search, Max knew he had hit a double (maybe a triple) right away. The first four results — *The Horror of Salisbury Prison, Salisbury Confederate POW Camp's Terrible Tragedy, North Carolina's Andersonville,* and *The Truth About North Carolina's Dark Secret in Salisbury.*

"Looks like you're about to tell me a whole lot," Max said to his laptop.

Though he put together a clear enough picture within a few

minutes, the full research lasted several hours. With four pages filled in his notebook, and a fifth with further rabbit holes he wanted to investigate, Max bathed in the flood of information — a rarity to enjoy.

According to the articles he read, the Salisbury Prison had been constructed early in 1861 as the war had been gearing up. The Confederates expected to capture a lot of Union soldiers and would need a secure place to house them. North Carolina offered to convert a sixteen-acre school campus into the prison (though some texts suggested in was an abandoned mill instead of a school). They planned to hold around twenty-five hundred inmates, and original designs suggested they hoped to create a model for humane treatment of enemy soldiers.

"In fact," Max said, "it looks like you succeeded. At first."

They had. By 1862, reports on Salisbury described prisoners as each having their own beds, access to decent food (edible, at least), and plenty of opportunities to fill their days with things to keep busy — a newspaper, prepared lectures, the chance to put on theatrical productions, and even a baseball team. And with the initial prisoner exchange program set up between the North and the South, it was easy to maintain a manageable prisoner population.

"But that won't last. There's a curse coming."

Problems began to mount on multiple fronts. First, the war was not going well for the South. What they thought was going to be a short matter in which they would whip the Yankees with ease had become a slog through a mire of bloody battlefields. The South had lost so many men they had to implement a draft. Doing so meant they would also have to enforce it, and that meant arresting deserters and draft dodgers. Many of those men wound up in Salisbury.

Another issue arose when the Union Army decided it no longer wanted to continue the prisoner exchanges. Too often Northern soldiers found themselves fighting with the same people they had captured only months earlier. By August 1864, General Grant had ended the exchange program. As a result, by October of the same year, Salisbury Prison held over five thousand people — twice its intended capacity. By the end of that same month, the number had swelled to nearly ten thousand prisoners.

Things turned ugly fast.

"I'll bet they did," Max muttered as he tried to find any crumb pointing to a curse.

Food shortages became regular matters and even the simplest of diseases would run rampant through the crowded population. Lack of adequate living space forced nearly seven thousand five hundred prisoners to sleep outside on the hard ground with night temperatures near freezing. Lice infestations were a non-stop problem and dozens died each day. A total of five thousand bodies were dumped in mass graves.

Max had to reread those numbers. Five thousand. Looking at the articles, he knew this was hardly the end of it all.

To maintain control, Major John Gee was brought in. The man had a harsh reputation, and the guards became stricter at every turn. With the guards grossly outnumbered and the prisoners grossly treated, some form of revolt was inevitable.

That moment came when Major Gee refused requests by the men to build their own makeshift shelters. Desperate, starving, and frozen, the prisoners plotted a mass escape. Because the guards lived outside the prison, they had to open the prison gate during each shift change. This was the opportunity the prisoners took advantage of.

On Friday, November 25, 1864 at 2pm, prisoners ambushed the new guards right after the shift change. They attacked with only sticks and rocks, but overwhelming numbers and desperation changed the odds. From those guards, they liberated better weapons. Two guards died from their own bayonets and many others were wounded. For a brief moment, those POWs must have thought they were going to succeed.

"But it all comes crashing down, doesn't it?"

The prisoners, in their feeble state, did not think through everything clearly. As a result, they huddled together as they tried to organize a storming of the gate. Hearing the commotion, the previous shift returned to find out what had happened, and upon seeing the situation, turned their muskets on the prisoners. Other guards brought out one of two cannons stationed at the prison. The big escape turned into a big massacre. Two hundred and fifty died. Another sixty wounded.

Despite restoring order, the end of it all neared. Three days after the South surrendered at Appomattox, General George Stoneman captured Salisbury, inspected the prison, freed all the men, and set the place ablaze.

Max sat back and absorbed the whole tale. He had to get up, walk through the house, shake off this horrid story and return to the present day. Because now he knew that Private Miller had been at Salisbury. He would have been a guard — possibly participated in the massacre of those prisoners attempting escape. Max also had the name of Miller's boss — Major John Gee.

The key piece still missing — any hint of witchcraft or other magic. No stories of weird, unexplained events. No mysterious deaths. Then again, when five thousand men were starving, freezing, and disease ridden, nobody took much notice of the actual cause of their deaths.

Max peeked in on Sandra, but she looked every bit as absorbed in her work as he knew he had been. Quietly he backed away into the kitchen and wrote her a note. He wanted to follow up his research in the library. If he was going to find the evidence he needed, his best bet was to look through primary sources — journals, military reports, and personal diaries. The Z. Smith Reynolds Library rarely failed him for those kinds of materials.

Chapter 24

EVEN AFTER ALL THESE YEARS, Max's chest still surged with hope when he stepped into the Z. Smith Reynolds Library. Whatever the problem, no matter how miniscule the lead, these halls of knowledge could provide the answer. But Max had to admit that surge did not feel so big this time. With a topic as enormous and well-researched as the Civil War, it bothered him that he did not get all the answers right away. Granted, the details of witchcraft used by Confederate soldiers in a lesser-known prison in rural North Carolina might not be as easily uncovered as the horrors of Andersonville or any number of major or minor battles, but information should have deluged him. The Civil War had been researched, written about, dissected, and debated since the day it started. Yet he found nothing about his specific question. If any place could help him, though, it was the Z. Smith Reynolds Library. He knew he had entered the realm of a gambler's superstitions, yet he still held onto that thinning bit of hope. He had to.

At least he knew where to start — Major John Gee.

Like most everything regarding the Civil War that did not involve witches or spells, Max had little trouble finding out about Major Gee. With one simple search, he put together a quick outline of the man. Before joining up with the Confederacy (not drafted like Miller), Major Gee was Dr. Gee. He worked in Florida as a physician, and if he had a sadistic bent, he kept it close to the vest.

However, like most wars, the Civil War had a way of bringing out the best and worst in a person. In Gee's case, given the authority to overlook POWs sparked the downright evil within. Perhaps, after the South surrendered, he returned to sanity.

Perhaps he tried to redeem himself. Or perhaps he spent his later years seeking ways to justify the harsh cruelty he inflicted upon his prisoners. Max chose not to investigate that much of the man unless it proved necessary.

He did find out that when the war ended, several war crimes trials occurred. Major Gee was the subject of one of them. The man must have seen it coming. Only weeks before, Captain Henry Wirz faced war crimes charges for his part as the Commandant of Andersonville. He was found guilty, and in November 1865, Wirz was hanged.

Major Gee was sadistic but not stupid. He had time to prepare his defense. Or run. But like many accused of war crimes, Gee did not see the wrong in anything he had done. The Confederacy had tasked him to maintain order in a prison vastly overcrowded and underfunded. As far as he could see, he performed an exemplary job. A Federal court in Raleigh, North Carolina agreed with him, noting that he had managed to handle numerous problems in an impossible situation. With his acquittal official, Gee returned to Florida, reclaimed his title of Doctor, and restarted his medical practice.

Max leaned his chair back and looked over his notes on Dr. Gee once more. He needed a word or phrase, a name or date, some clue to point him toward his next step. Setting his notes down, he gazed up at the ceiling.

The Z. Smith Reynolds Library was actually two older buildings that had been joined into one by walling up the gap between them. The library designers covered the gap with a roof that let the sunlight in, and therefore, left the area open. Several stories of open light shone down on a workspace of desks below. On either side, the various floors ended in balconies overlooking this space, and the overall effect was simultaneously grandiose and cozy.

Max thought the same of Salisbury. The story was both oversized and sadly personal — a huge tragedy, an uprising and horrible quelling, but also the thousands of individual stories of struggle that Max could get lost in, if he allowed himself the time to research them all. And somewhere hidden among those thousands, an answer awaited.

Gazing around the library, he noticed the emptiness. On a Sunday, there should have been plenty of students. Of course, some were hungover from college parties, and many preferred using their computers to access the library rather than come in person. Which meant the one unique resource the library had which could not be found online was completely available to him without having to wait at all — the librarian.

"Excuse me," Max said as he approached the main counter. "I'm looking for primary documents regarding the Salisbury prison from the Civil War. Can you help me?"

The librarian, Mrs. Ivy Meyer, smiled from behind large glasses chained around her neck. "Have you searched the computer for call numbers yet?"

"Not yet. That is — I'm familiar with using the special documents room, but without searching, I already know there must be at least two or three thousand possible documents. But most will be from other libraries, and I don't have the time to wait on an inter-library loan. I was hoping you could save me a lot of trouble if you knew or could find out exactly what this library held."

"I'll be happy to do so. Wait here, please."

She went off to a back room — probably to call up the special documents floor. Max could have discovered all this information on his own, but the one thing a living librarian brought that made this a worthwhile avenue — human intuition. Sure enough, she came back with a paper and a quizzical frown.

"This is a list of what we have," she said, handing over the printout.

"But?"

"It seems rather small. I know we've had much larger holdings in the past. And I don't that mean long ago. Just a few months."

"What does that mean? The library wouldn't get rid of them. Not primary sources."

"Never. And sources from the Civil War would not be allowed to leave this building in general. Though it's possible a professor at another university has taken them on loan for research purposes, but I find it hard to believe we would let someone, even a scholar, take more than two or three items at one time." She tapped her fingernail against her teeth. "Do you mind waiting a bit longer? I want to check on something."

"Please do. I appreciate it."

As the librarian headed away again, Max's stomach sank. Outside of a university professor, Max could think of only one person with enough clout to take these documents — Cecily Hull. No doubt, on behalf of Madame Ti. They must have been planning this for months. Miller wasn't drawn to J's abilities. Rather, he targeted J at Madame Ti's insistence. They used J to get Max and Sandra and Drummond to bring it all together, find the location on Graveyard Island, and help cast the spell that raised the spirit.

"I thought so," Mrs. Meyer said as she returned. "I noticed a marking on each of these titles which didn't make sense. I just double-checked with one of the other librarians and it turns out somebody must have changed the coding system we've been using. We have a new head librarian, and whenever that happens, the old ways are supposedly improved."

Max offered a sympathetic chuckle. "Too many people have never heard the saying *if ain't broke, don't fix it.*"

"Ain't that the truth. Anyway, this listing is not what I said — not documents taken out of this building. Instead, they've been recently requested, viewed, and returned, but they have yet to be reshelved."

She handed over the list as Max's pulse perked up. A quick scan down the page spotted two important names. First, he saw that the list included the name of the person who had requested these documents. That information should have been removed before giving him the printout, but Mrs. Meyer appeared to have forgotten. And from that mistake, Max saw the name *Paulson Carroll.*

Mr. Carroll, new head of the Brotherhood of the Rising, and an individual with a particular interest in summoning spirits. Apparently, Madame Ti wasn't as paranoid about the

Brotherhood as Max had thought. Carroll would not be happy when he learned she beat him to this particular spirit.

The second name, however, meant more in the short term. It sat near the bottom of the documents list and had not been taken out in over twenty years. Certainly not by Mr. Carroll. The full title of the document — *the final journal of Captain Arnold Getty, Union Army.* Max had been so caught up in seeking Confederate connections to Miller, he forgot the most obvious connection — a Union prisoner.

About fifteen minutes later, Max sat at a lovely wood-carved table in the quiet, near-empty special documents room and waited for the Documents Assistant to bring out the requested journal. While the regular soldiers would have been hard-pressed to find paper and quill for journal writing — if they were literate enough to write — the officers were granted added privileges. From what Max could find on the original layout of the prison, the Union officers had even been kept separated from their men.

On the surface, this appeared to be a matter of classism. Indeed, the officers had larger quarters and better food — still meager in both categories but better than their men. However, Max suspected the separation was also a means of preventing the officers from leading a rebellion. Which, in fact, they did after overcrowding destroyed all sense of rank or class.

Another five minutes went by, and as Max arched back to see if he could spot the assistant, the young lady returned with Captain Getty's journal — a series of once-crumpled papers written in a jagged script. Each paper had been sleeved in protective plastic, and the sleeves had been bound in a large book designed to keep the pages flat and safe. Still, the library required Max to wear a set of latex gloves before handling the pages.

A typed index card had been placed in the front sleeve explaining that the pages had been discovered by Jenna Coleman in April 1972 while touring the Salisbury National Cemetery — built on the remains of the destroyed prison with the mass graves as a memorial to this dark chapter. Apparently, Ms. Coleman had come across a line of stonework she thought might be original to the prison and while poking around it, found the pages rolled tight and placed in a hole near the bottom.

Max turned to the first page. The edges on the top were charred slightly from the final days of the war when General Stoneman had the prison burned. Max read:

> *September 21, 1864*
> *Whomever may find it worthwhile to read these words should not expect an accounting of the foul indignities we are suffering at the hands of the Confederacy and in particular, Major John Gee. My fellow officers are taking great lengths to make sure such documentation is properly performed and I trust them to diligently leave any and all that is required. My purpose here is not to provide any information at all, but rather to explain what I intend to do, why and how, in hopes that, should I succeed, should there be truth in the fantastical possibilities of what I have been led to believe, then perhaps I can be forgiven. Perhaps my soul will not be eternally tarnished.*

Even if Captain Getty's preamble had not been so pointed, Max's instincts fired hot enough to know he had finally come across what he needed. Were there any doubt, it swept away with the next part of the journal.

> *I first met the Witch after a short but brutal confrontation in the backwoods of North Carolina. I led a small scouting unit of four and we happened upon an equal four Rebs relieving themselves in a creek. Each man managed a shot or two depending on weaponry, and as might be expected should the reader hold a knowledge of warfare, matters devolved into bayonets, hunting knives, rocks, and fists. Anything at hand became a deadly weapon.*
>
> *At the conclusion, I rested at the base of a tree, blood dripping from my chest and arms and legs. All seven other soldiers had perished. Despite my years upon the battlefield, I had never before witnessed such animalistic*

brutality as in those several few minutes. And I found myself alone and feeling a desperate urge to curse and wail. The Witch arrived like a scavenging beast and I hissed at her. A true hiss like a snake warning off a threat. Only she did not flee. She squatted as if to foul the creek and she stared at me. No, it was more than that. She stared into me. Through me. She gripped me with fear and I could not move.

"I will give you the means to avenge your men," she said to me with her serpent eyes and goat tongue. I recall every word as if she whispers them into my ear this very minute. I shall never forget. "I will show you the mighty symbols and how to use them. Only once can you do so and only the once. When your heart is ravaged with hatred for your enemy you must strike. Do you want this?"

Of course, Getty wanted it. He wouldn't have told the tale if he had let the witch be on her way. Beyond the obvious, though, Max noticed the hurried, feverish way the man wrote — scrawled, really — as if he knew the prisoners only had months, maybe days left to live.

Carefully, Max turned to the next page. He wanted to talk to the journal, to Getty, but the extra quiet in the Special Documents Room and his own growing tension kept his mouth sealed.

I won't explain here why I agreed. Vengeance against Gee and all of his men is partly to blame, but that came later, and yet if I am to be fully honest in these pages, then I would have to faithfully tell the long narrative of my life, of all the wrongs done to and by myself, and I have not been provided enough paper for such a journey. As far as I can imagine, it does not matter. I told the Witch I should agree to her terms and she would provide the spell.

For Max, that paragraph guaranteed the authenticity of this

document. If Captain Getty had concocted a fiction to amuse himself in his troubled final days or if he had lost his mind in the duress of his situation and merely rambled on the page or any number of other possibilities leading to the journal being a lie, he would have provided details of the deal he made. Hinted at them, at least. The fact that Getty hid this proved its truth — the kind of payment a witch would want for such a spell would be the kind of thing no sane person would want to admit on paper.

I returned to the same spot for a week. The same tree by the same creek. My superiors thought I mourned the loss of my unit and required the time there to digest with the viciousness of the hard-fought battle. There was some truth in that regard, but mostly, I returned to see the Witch each day, so she could teach me the symbols and how to use them.

Learning the proper form of the drawing was simple, at first, but required such exacting sizes, shapes, and motions that the Witch grew impatient with me, at times. One also had to recite short phrases in languages I have never heard and pray I never hear again. The words, when spoken, felt evil on the tongue and shaped the mouth with a filthy sensation. After seven grueling days, she finally said I knew the spell well enough, took her payment, and returned to whatever foul Hell she came from.

She told me the name of this cursed magic, but even thinking the name chills my body. I choose to call it the Demon's Curse and that will suffice. And I have chosen this day to finally use the spell. I shall write the symbols on my last paper, and I shall avenge all those who have fallen before me, and I shall avenge all of us which will perish in the days ahead.

Do not fear the symbols here. Without word or intention or the blood in my veins, the writing has no power within

> *it. You shall not be harmed by gazing upon it and it will not provide you any special gift should you foolishly attempt to use it. When I have completed my task, I will place these pages in a secure location and pray that someday they will be found, read, and understood. I pray I will be forgiven.*

Knowing the shake in his fingers came from both anxiety and anticipation, Max turned to the final page. It showed the least damage of the entire journal, and he suspected it had been rolled closest to the center. Or perhaps that magic infused in the spell had also protected it.

Like the other symbols they were dealing with, the main one looked like an amalgamation of pieces. Max recognized the two arches like the top half of a heart — a symbol common enough that he had seen it in several of Sandra's spells. He thought he could make out some jagged lines that looked familiar, but he could have been mistaken.

He glanced around the empty room to make sure nobody watched him. Then he pulled out his phone — dried out and thankfully functional — checked that the flash was off, and snapped several pictures of the symbol. Cycling through the results, he sent the best one to Sandra, adding a text: *Possibly used on Miller. See what you can find.*

As he returned the document to the desk and waited for the elevator, his phone vibrated. Sandra responded: *Call me. I can tell you all about it.*

Chapter 25

AS HE TRUDGED OFF TO HIS CAR, another rain shower opened up. The car engine didn't turn over. He tried two more times before it finally caught. The next case better pay them well because they couldn't afford to fix this car. He called Sandra, put the phone on speaker and headed out.

After Max explained about Captain Getty, Sandra said, "This is starting to make some sense."

"That sounds like you found out something. Tell me."

"I'd rather you focus on the road. I'll tell you when you get home."

"I haven't slept well in days. Talk with me. Keep me awake."

"Fine, but if the rain gets harder, promise me you'll pull over."

"I promise. Now start talking. What are those symbols Getty drew all about?"

"The key one is a variant of the main symbol in Madame Ti's spell, but more importantly, it's a combination of witchcraft and far older pagan spells."

Max turned the windshield wipers to full. "We expected that, right? The Brotherhood used magic older than witchcraft in order to summon an inhuman spirit."

"Yes, but by combining the spell with witchcraft, I had a chance of narrowing down the origins. Some spells have characteristics that reveal who created it. Think of it like a signature. Mother Hope always used the double-wave line in the southern compass point of her spells. That symbol added nothing but she did it anyway. I'm sure Grandma Mobley also had a similar symbol she used, though I never had a chance to examine her personal work in great detail. Really, any strong witch will have developed a personal voice to the way they write a spell."

"Even Madame Ti?"

"Definitely. But the spell she cast for the inhuman spirit, Wardarit, is not of her making. In fact, the key shape — the signature part — matches a series of spells I uncovered on one of my private witch sites. It also matches what you sent me."

Max pulled to the curb and turned on his hazard lights. The rain drummed hard on the roof of his car. He needed to think. "You're saying that the spell Madame Ti used was designed by the same witch who made a deal with Captain Getty?"

"There's no doubt that Madame Ti chose those symbols because of that connection. It has to be."

"Then this witch used Getty to summon a spirit? But if she had the spell already, why risk using a novice? And what benefit is there for her when Getty would be the one who got to make a deal with the spirit? It makes no sense."

"You're forgetting what Irene said. Not all spirits are summoned to make a Devil's Bargain. That was what happened in the other case because the Brotherhood wanted to gain power quickly. In this case, I don't think the witch intended to ask for anything. I think she might have been using Getty as a guinea pig."

"Testing out if her spell would work?"

"Sure. No other witch would ever agree to do the honors for her — they all know how dangerous a spirit can be."

"Not all witches know about spirits. You didn't."

"Those that didn't know would still be wary of a fellow witch offering her spell to be used. It doesn't happen like that."

A small truck zipped by splashing a wave of dirty water over the car. "I still don't understand why she would use Getty. What good is testing a spell, if the tester had never cast a spell before, had almost zero chance of being able to cast anything at all?"

"I don't know. Maybe she thought it was easy enough."

"A spell to summon a spirit? Easy?"

"You said she spent a week going through every detail with the man, so clearly she worked to prepare him to succeed. And summoning spirits is not looked upon favorably in most witch communities." As Sandra spoke, the distinct clack of her keyboard could be heard. "Hold on. This is interesting."

"What's that?"

"Shush. Just wait."

Max played out Captain Getty's story in his head like a mini-movie. He saw the brutal battle and the loss of everyone but Getty. He saw Getty collapse against the tree by the creek, the man's face locked in shock. He saw the witch approach and make her offer. Max tried to see a reason for the witch to do so, but he failed. The 1860s were not a period in history known for their grand acceptance of witches. Why would this one be okay exposing her existence to this Union solider?

"Got her," Sandra said.

"What? How?"

"You're not going to like this. I used Google. Score one for my simple but effective search techniques." She laughed. Perhaps hearing Max's grinding teeth, she went on, "It was difficult using the witch websites to get information about the symbols for identity purposes. While we were talking, I decided to google the symbols and several images of gravestones came up. That got me thinking —"

Feeling an excited surge of energy, Max slapped the steering wheel. "The one we found on Graveyard Island."

"Yeah. I checked the photos you took of that witch's grave. The signature symbol is a perfect match. The witch who designed the spell and gave it to Captain Getty — her name was Delilah French."

Max pulled back into traffic. "Honey, you're the greatest there is or ever was."

"I know."

"I'll be home later than planned."

"Where are you going now?"

"Only place that makes any sense to me at the moment — Salisbury. I've got to see where this all happened. Figure out what this witch was really after."

"Okay. I'll do what I can on this end. Now that we have her name, I should be able to find a lot more. Especially if she was part of a coven."

"See you for dinner tonight."

"I love you, hon. Please, be careful."

"I will, but don't worry. It's a rainy Sunday afternoon at a national cemetery. Not exactly a high crime situation."

"Are you trying to jinx yourself?"

Max chuckled.

Chapter 26

UPON REACHING SALISBURY, Max pulled up the government website for national cemeteries. Bouncing between the rough diagrams of the cemetery layout and the phone's map program, Max expertly got lost. Turned out there were two cemeteries on opposite sides of the town — the Salisbury National Cemetery and the Historic Salisbury National Cemetery. That one extra word made a huge difference, and while he eventually found his way to Government Road which wound to a closed circle at the end, he wasted too much time in the process.

Tucked between a suburban neighborhood on one side and an industrial area on the other, the historic version of the cemetery had been built upon the former prison lands (the other cemetery sat behind the VA hospital). Tall trees blocked the industrial area and muted some of the noise. But still the sounds of air compressors, drills, and saws rolled along the air as well as the rumble of a train rushing down tracks opposite the main gate of the cemetery.

Even in death, these poor soldiers seem cursed.

With military precision, identical white gravestones filled the manicured grass in perfect rows and columns. The dead laid out at attention. Flower arrangements adorned some of the graves while others had stones placed upon the top.

Max parked near a tall flagpole. A large American flag hung limp in the still air. Nearby, he found several angled stands with metal plates bolted on. One bore a map of the area, showing the various burial plots and their corresponding numbers. The plate read:

BURIAL TRENCHES AND SALISBURY PRISON

You are facing the 18 trenches used by the Salisbury Confederate Prison for the burial of prisoners, most of whom died after October 1864

To the right of the this rather clinical description, Max recognized that the long lines on the simplistic map the burial plots surrounded were the trenches. The mass graves of around five thousand men. They encompassed a swath of land that seemed both enormous and not enormous enough. Not for five thousand.

He stared at the flat grass field — still as the air. Yet if Sandra or Drummond or J were here, they would be able to tell him about the crowded mass of ghosts overwhelming these trenches. He guessed that should he walk across that open field he would suffer one icy touch after another. The air was probably in a permanent state of cold.

Given that Captain Getty was an officer, Max thought there was a good chance the man had been given an actual grave instead of being thrown into the trenches. If he had been part of the mass grave, the likelihood of finding him went to nearly zero. Unless Sandra wanted to cast a spell, but considering their current streak of luck with mixing Civil War graves, bones, and magic, Max did not think it would be a good gamble.

"Might as well get to it," he muttered as he pulled out his phone.

There truly existed an app for everything, and Max had recently downloaded one called Find-a-Grave. Seemed prudent. He tapped in the cemetery name and the name of the deceased. In seconds, he learned that Getty had indeed been buried on his own in Plot 4. The app highlighted the grave marker and drew a somber dark-green line from where Max stood to the grave — set in the back, behind a large magnolia tree.

Walking by row after row of lost lives, Max tried to imagine how Captain Getty must have felt through it all. Even before his imprisonment, he had experienced the brutal horrors of war.

They had a profound touch upon him — enough so that he willingly made a deal with a witch. And then the strange part. He held onto this spell throughout the war. Probably came close to using it numerous times but stopped himself. Why?

The witch had warned him he could only use the spell once. Might even have been true considering his amateur level of ability. In fact, Max pictured Getty going to sleep every night reciting the words, going through the motions of drawing the symbol, memorizing his own memorization until he could see each individual line in its purest, most perfect form.

Yet after his capture, after seeing the horrid conditions under which the Union POWs lived, he still held back. Something kept him from enacting that spell. It wasn't until his own death neared, when he knew there would never be another opportunity, when conditions at Salisbury had reached such an abysmal state that casting a spell seemed a reasonable action — only then did Getty act.

As Max rounded the wide trunk, he saw a square of white gravestones. Standing next to one near the back, a woman in flowing black robes stood with her head bowed and her arms out. Though he could not see her face, Max knew without doubt who he stared at — Madame Ti.

Damn. He juggled too many loose pieces at the moment. He knew the events in broad strokes but had no idea how they all fit together. A lack of information equaled standing on shaky ground. Not a good position to be in when dealing with the head witch under any circumstance — but especially under their current ones.

He paused by the tree. She was either doing some odd standing meditation or casting a spell. Max guessed the latter. With her concentration focused on that task, he could slip back to his car and drive off without her ever knowing he had been so nearby. Go home, have dinner with Sandra and the boys, then return later in the evening. If the gates were closed, he could climb the fence. Wouldn't be the first time he broke into a cemetery.

Only problem with that plan — by the time he returned to

Captain Getty's grave, Madame Ti would have accomplished whatever she set out to do. Since her spell undoubtedly had some connection to Miller and the spirit Wardarit, he could not afford to give her a further lead — even if he didn't know exactly what they were racing towards.

Clearing his throat, Max strode toward her with his hands casually in his pockets — his right firmly gripping the empty 9mm. "I would have thought you'd still be on Graveyard Island playing with your new friend." He continued his approach.

Madame Ti lifted her head and glanced back with a sly lick of the lips. "Why now, Mr. Porter, I cannot say I'm surprised to see you here. In fact, I had a bit of fear that you may have gotten here before I did. I'm happy to see I was wrong on that count."

"You've already raised an inhuman spirit and gotten control of the thing. You've already locked that spirit to Miller's ghost and that of his friends. Isn't that enough for you? Why do you want to bother with Getty?"

Lowering her arms, she faced Max. "I keep forgetting — you're not so smart. Do you really think I have the power to summon a spirit?"

"Doesn't seem that hard. A bunch of novices like the Brotherhood managed it."

"And look how that turned out. It's not enough to know the spell or speak the words or draw the proper symbols. That might succeed in unleashing a spirit, but in order for any of it to be useful, a witch has to be able to summon and control what she has summoned. That's the hard part. Control. Without it, there's no point to trying in the first place."

"You want me to believe that Wardarit was already summoned? That it was by chance we needed your help with a ghost that had an inhuman spirit locked to it?"

"That would be absurd."

"Then why not enlighten me? I'm truly interested in how a dead Confederate soldier singled out my son and led us down a path which resulted in you controlling an inhuman spirit."

"Isn't it obvious? I set it all up."

Max halted. He had suspected as much but didn't think she

would ever admit it. Something else wriggled at the back of his thoughts — Ruby. Where was she?

Before he even finished thinking her name, he heard her approaching fast from behind. Whirling to face her — slick, black-haired version of her — he managed to whip the 9mm from his pocket. But taking aim while pretending the weapon was loaded caused him to lose focus on the actual attack — rookie mistake. Ruby bashed his wrist, sending the weapon flipping over into the grass. He raised his arms and rolled his fingers into tight fists. But none of that was fast enough to stop the blow to his head.

The world loop-de-looped and he felt the cold ground chilling the side of his face. Wobbling to his hands and knees, he pushed hard to get standing. He only had seconds before she — but even that thought took too long. Ruby pressed her knee on his back, flattening him back to the ground. He felt a sharp prick on his neck.

"What is that?" Madame Ti asked.

"Nothing dangerous," Ruby said. "Just a sedative."

He heard Madame Ti and Ruby continue their conversation, but the words mutated into collections of sounds with no meaning. Ruby grabbed him under the arms and dragged him toward the parking area. A soft, pleasant movement across the grass of the dead. He smiled. Last thing he noticed before passing out — she dug his keys out of his pocket.

Chapter 27

AWAKENING TO A DRY MOUTH and pounding headache always reminded Max of college hangovers. But in those days, he would open his gluey eyes to find his dorm room, a friend's apartment, or on a few occasions, a lovely co-ed's bed. This was his first hangover waking up underground with the smell of a sewer permeating the air.

He sat in a low, gray metal office chair situated in the middle of a utility room. Chain link fence formed one wall. Stacks of boxes covered two of the other walls. And the last one had a gray metal office desk, four gray metal file cabinets, a work table with some basic tools scattered about, a calendar mounted above the table, and a Playboy centerfold taped next to it. A bare yellow bulb hung from the center of the ceiling.

Max pressed on the chair's arms to sit straighter and found no resistance — he was not tied up. He bent forward and checked his legs. No ropes, no chains. Nothing to keep him from running. Well, almost nothing. He did see that a salt circle had been drawn around the chair, and while that could not stop him, it did not bode well for his future. But what truly forced him to stay seated — aside from the terrible ache parading through his head — was the woman with her back against the fencing. Ruby. Auburn hair this time.

"Well, well," she said, with a strange accent — an attempt at Eastern European from World War II. It would have been comical, if not for the reality of the moment and the pain in his wrist to remind him that this woman could be quite dangerous. "Finally awake."

"Little water, please."

"Of course. Where are my manners?" Ruby crossed the room

to a sink in the back corner that Max had missed. She wore a gray suit like a cop and held her jaw forward as if she had been born with a different bone structure. When she returned with a plastic cup of water, she handed it over and backed away. "You had me a tad worried. I've not administered a shot like that before, and certainly not under such strenuous circumstances. I thought I might have killed you."

"No such luck. Just made me feel terrible."

Revealing her teeth, she said, "There's always next time."

Max noted that she carried a sidearm in a shoulder holster. "What is it with you? Is this some kind of cos-play thing or do you really suffer from multiple personalities? For a short while, I thought you might have a twin. I guess that could still be true. Just curious. What's the answer?"

"I ask the questions. You answer them. Otherwise, you stay quiet."

"Okay, okay. Go ahead. What do you want to ask me? Oops. Sorry. That was another question."

Ruby's nostrils flared and she backhanded him. With the side of his face stinging, he squeezed his eyes shut until he could refocus. Then he heard the sharp click of heels.

Madame Ti entered the room, rolled a chair up close, and sat. She never stopped grinning. "I apologize for the rather harsh methods we've been forced to employ in getting you here. I'm sure you understand."

"Of course," Max said, rubbing his cheek. "Though I find this room not nearly as nice as your office. Can't say the smell is much different."

"You speak to her with respect." Ruby raised her hand once more.

Madame Ti crossed her legs and waved Ruby back. "I think Mr. Porter is quite aware of how to speak to me. Beating him won't change anything. However, he'll be a far more decent person to converse with once he understands his true predicament."

Max spit a little blood to the side. "And now come the threats."

"Let us begin with Captain Getty's bones. I want to know how you took them and where they are now."

"I didn't take them. I would have had to dig a huge hole and — are you saying you tried a spell to raise his bones, but they weren't there?"

With a patient sigh, Madame Ti gestured to Ruby. The auburn woman launched forward and punched Max in the gut. As he bent forward, she shoved his chin up and back. Then she slapped his face hard enough to redden the skin as if he had a sunburn.

"That's plenty," Madame Ti said, and Ruby backed off into the shadows. "You might do better tonight if you take Ruby's earlier advice — we do the asking; you do the answering."

Blood dripped off the corner of Max's lip and some slipped into his mouth. He nodded.

"Excellent. Then I'll ask again. Where did you take Captain Getty's bones?"

"When I walked up to you at that grave, it was the first time I'd ever been there."

Ruby moved in, but Madame Ti stopped her. "Not everything is easily solved with your fists."

The auburn pugilist smirked. "Most things."

Closing her eyes, Madame Ti lifted her hand as if warning Max to halt. Her flat palm shimmered a dull, pale light as she made odd croaking vocalizations. Smoke rose from the salt circle around him, and he could hear it crackling like a campfire.

Her brow lowered and her hand quivered. He felt heat building up in his right pants pocket — Sandra's ward. Hiding any sign of hope, he looked at the floor and waited. With a sudden sigh, Madame Ti dropped her hand.

"Well?" Ruby asked.

"I think he's telling the truth."

"You're not sure?"

"I've cast a lot of spells today. Difficult ones. That requires a lot of energy. I'm not at my best at the moment, so yes — all I can say is that he is most likely telling the truth."

Max couldn't hold his tongue. "See?" he said, and Ruby exercised great restraint in not punching him again.

The witch stood, keeping steady with one hand on the chair. "This is good news for you, Mr. Porter. Since you have not interfered with Captain Getty, you can go home."

"I can?"

"Your case is over. You wanted to free your son from being tethered to a ghost. That's why you came to me, after all. And I delivered, as promised. J Porter is free. Private Miller has been reunited with his remains. Any other matters surrounding the events on Graveyard Island do not concern you."

He quelled the urge to stand so that he could look downward at her. Ruby's hungry glower provided all the incentive he needed to stay put. Rubbing his sore lips, he said, "It's been my experience that when people say something doesn't concern me, it probably concerns me. Especially when the warning comes from a witch. Double-especially when that witch is playing around with inhuman spirits."

"I see. You are worried about Wardarit, but you needn't be. That inhuman spirit will not be locked to those old ghosts for much longer. Once freed, Private Miller and his fellow soldiers will be able to move on in peace." She turned away and walked by Ruby. "That is why I'm advising you to return home and put all this to rest. I'm sure Sandra and J and the other one would much prefer that you were there."

Max forced a laugh, making sure to spread on a thick helping of mockery. She had already revealed more than she should — enough that Max had started to see a bit of the truth — and if he could keep her off balance, then perhaps he would learn everything. Or get another punch in the gut. He gave the plan a 50-50 chance.

Madame Ti folded her arms across her chest as if giving herself a hug. "Am I wrong about your family? Don't they want you home?"

"They do." He dabbed at his eyes. "I'm not laughing at that."

"Then what?"

"The fact that you're scared. Wardarit frightens you."

"Only an idiot doesn't fear an inhuman spirit. They are unstable, vicious creatures."

While true, Max knew there was more going on with her. And it started with that inhuman spirit. Ever since Graveyard Island, Max had assumed Madame Ti was the one to lock the spirit to Miller's ghost. He figured that the second spell she and Sandra performed that night was responsible. After Max and his team swam into the lake and escaped, he assumed Madame Ti had taken control of Wardarit.

But she had just said that Miller and his friends were not free of the spirit yet. That meant she did not control it. Not enough, anyway. Not the kind of control that would let her decimate her enemies. *Of which, I'm probably one.*

Even more important, he caught her attempting to get ahold of Captain Getty's bones. Yet there were no bones in the grave, and she assumed Max had stolen them. Those facts held a lot of implications.

"You can't control this spirit," he said as the thought formed. "Probably can't even reach it."

Ruby rushed forward. "You watch your mouth. Madame Ti is the most powerful —"

"It's okay," Madame Ti said, ushering Ruby back a few steps. "I'm not afraid of his words."

While Ruby paced near the chain link fence like a zoo lioness itching to feed on the people watching her, Madame Ti defied Max with her glare as if daring him to continue. He gave two seconds of thought to it before barreling ahead. "The only reason you would be poking around Getty's grave is because you know about the witch he met and the spell he cast. What are you thinking? You have some spell that will let you dominate an inhuman spirit with those bones? That would mean that Getty actually summoned the thing, right? Otherwise, his specific bones would hold no sway over Wardarit."

As the words left his mouth, he saw how Getty must have used the witch's spell in a last, desperate attempt to save his men and himself. Or perhaps a final attack against his enemy, no matter the consequences.

"He doesn't understand," Madame Ti said to Ruby before turning back. "After all I've done to stabilize the witch community, to rein in the use of magic in the state, to create a safe environment for both witch and non-witch, one where we can coexist in peace, and you have the gall to question me as if I'm some hook-nosed, wart festering witch of legend."

"Doesn't seem like you're succeeding. Everywhere I look, the witches are acting like nobody's in charge."

"That won't last much longer. Your wife and I — we're among the few good witches out there. We're the ones trying to fix the power-hungry mess. But it doesn't happen overnight, and it doesn't happen without some pain. Punishments must be served. Justice must be enacted. If those who have abused or failed our system are permitted to live on without any real form of atonement, then they'll simply go on repeating the same vicious cycle. Do you understand now?"

Max felt a tinge of pity. "You really believe that, don't you? You've convinced yourself that using horrifying magic to summon these vile spirits is justified."

"You mistake me. I want to create a balanced and just witch society that can live right next to the non-witch one. Cecily Hull agrees with me — that this would be the best way for us all to live on in peace. Even if the non-witches have no idea. But she is not taking the threat of the Brotherhood seriously. So, I must."

"And that means dealing with inhuman spirits?"

"Fight fire with fire. Quite frankly, I'm mystified you don't want them to suffer. They are the ones who tried to have you possessed by a spirit, after all."

"Forgive me for not being all-in with you, but I've seen what a spirit can do. It's best to let those things stay wherever they're from. They don't belong in our world."

"I do agree with your last point. But this one is here and I need to use it for a bit before letting it go home."

"You're nuts if you think you can control it."

Ruby charged right up and decked him. Flashes of light burst into his vision, and Max knew he'd have a black eye by morning. He wasn't sure if she had broken his nose, too, but it hurt enough to convince him of the possibility.

"Stop," Madame Ti said as Ruby pulled back her fist for

another pounding.

"You can't let him talk to you like that. I've known too many men like him. They only understand violence."

"Ruby, dear, I appreciate these gestures, but they are unnecessary." She placed a hand on Ruby's shoulder before turning her cold eyes on Max. "I am a strong, powerful witch. I don't need my fists in order to get what I want. I simply need the truth. Mr. Porter here understands that. He looks into my eyes, and he knows that no matter what he thinks he has learned, the most important lesson of the night is this — the Porter Agency will close the Miller case. There will be no more inquiries into this matter, and while I found our discussion of inhuman spirits entertaining, they will not pursue that or any aspect of such things anymore." With a crooked finger, she pointed at Max. "Because if you continue to interfere, then when I do control Wardarit, I'll see that it feasts on your entire family. Not just Sandra and J. But the other boy and your mother, too. And when the spirit is done with them, I'll have it run down your ghost friend and tear him to pieces. You'll be last, of course, and you'll die having watched all that you love suffer and end." She paused. Then: "No witty remark?"

Max had witnessed a lot of terrible sights, but Madame Ti's dead eyes were among the worst. He searched for a glint of humanity, something to convince him she was bluffing or at least exaggerating. Instead, he saw conviction and naked ambition.

"Good," she said. "See, Ruby — I do believe Mr. Porter is starting to learn a little respect." With a light lilt suddenly invading her voice, she headed to the exit. "It's getting late and we all have places to be. Be a dear, Ruby, and escort our guest to his car. Try not to bruise him any further."

"No promises."

"Mr. Porter, let us hope we do not see each other again. At least, not until I call in on our previous deal. Good night."

As she walked away to the rhythm of her clicking heels, Max half-expected her to cackle like a movie villain. Ruby decided to fulfill that part. However, she opted for the slow and low chuckle full of menace.

"Get up," she said.

Flinching at her approach, Max's eye pulsed with a promise of being swollen and sore for a week. "I got the message. You don't have to —"

"Hurt you? Beat you? But darling — I want to." Her sickening glee made her look more insane than all the personality changes combined.

Until her mouth snapped wide open and her eyes glazed in queasy confusion. Her muscles spasmed and she dropped to the floor. Marshall Drummond floated behind her — his hand still in the air where he had thrust it into her head and froze her unconsciousness.

"Do you have any idea how hard it is to find a person in this maze?" he said. "Sewer tunnels, witch-layer tunnels — the place is a labyrinth."

Max bolted to his feet, wanting to give Drummond a hug and knowing he couldn't. "Thank you."

"Don't get all weepy."

"All I said was —"

"Okay, I can see your adoration overwhelming your common sense. Let's get out of here first, then you can praise me all you want on the drive home."

"The drive," Max said and rushed over to Ruby. He patted her down until he found the lump in her denim jacket — his car keys. "Was it dumb luck you found me, or do you know how to get back to the surface?"

"And the praise goes out the window. *Dumb luck?* You think I've just been wandering in circles until I stumbled upon you? I'll have you know that I took a systematic approach to —"

"We don't have time. Can you get us out?"

Drummond flicked the brim of his hat. "Of course. Follow me."

Chapter 28

EACH UNSTEADY STEP along the city sidewalks brought Max closer to feeling safe. Once he reached his car, once he drove toward Sandra and the boys, he shuddered off the anxiety from being held by a witch. Though not the first time, the experience never got easier. But anytime he ended up in some dank room with a witch looming over him meant his life could end. Or worse.

Max pressed harder on the gas. Ruby had swiped his phone — probably in hopes of finding pictures of Getty's bones. Instead, she got a barely useable waterlogged device. Now phoneless, Max asked Drummond to dash on ahead and let Sandra know all was well. That gave Max a moment of privacy. One he used to shout and wail and bellow. He used it to slap the steering wheel and bang his back into the seat.

When he finally reached home, Sandra burst out as he stepped from the car. The shock on her face told him how bad his bruises looked, but thankfully that did not stop her for long. She flung her arms around him, and all the anger and fear and frustration of Madame Ti and Ruby dissipated beneath her strong grip. If only for a moment.

At length, they went to their bedroom, closed the door, and Max explained what had happened while Drummond and Sandra listened. The Sandwich Boys were both asleep — partly because they had school in the morning; partly because they were teenagers and mostly ate or slept. Max checked the clock on the dresser — 11:21pm. Still Sunday night and not nearly as late as he had expected.

Propped up against the headboard, he popped four ibuprofen and held Sandra in his arms as he recounted all the details. His legs itched to pace the room, but the rest of him locked around her and refused to let go. At short intervals, he would pause to kiss the top of her head, or when she glanced up, kiss her on the mouth. Each time, his body flooded with the reassurance, the confidence, the strength, the love that they've always instilled in each other. It was the one constant that offered them any protection from a spirit. Their personal ward.

When he hit the point of his story where Drummond saved him from another beating, the others held silent. Sandra's arms slipped tighter around his waist. The silence continued.

"I know," Max finally said. "I feel the same way — that we don't know what to do. Part of me wants to jump into the middle and start punching. Fight back against all of this. Part of me thinks we should do what Madame Ti wants. Back off and take the win. We freed J from Miller. The rest doesn't have to be our problem."

Drummond pursed his lips as he considered Max's words. "Except if Madame Ti goes on to get control of that spirit, it will become our problem — and a much bigger one."

"That's why part of me thinks we need to handle this now. We must be close to the truth. They wouldn't have come down hard on me, they wouldn't have done anything at all to me, if we had no hope of finding out what's going on and being able to stop it."

Sandra said, "It does seem like she's worried about you getting in the way."

"The problem for me is that part of me thinks we're not ready to fight a witch like Madame Ti. We barely know anything about her. When we took on Grandma Mobley and Mother Hope, we had been involved with them for years. They were no strangers and we knew a lot of their tactics. Even their weaknesses. But we don't have the time now to look into Madame Ti."

"We've had plenty of it," Drummond said. "Let's be honest. We all hoped that things would be different under Cecily Hull. Not perfect, not even close, but different. Seems to me like we're heading down that old familiar path of power-grabbing and trying to control people."

Careful to avoid causing Max any pain, Sandra pushed up to sit. "No use whining about a bunch of should'ves and could'ves. We're here now, and we've got to deal with it."

"But that's really it," Max said. Then: "Maybe we don't have to deal with it. Maybe we should put the safety of the Sandwich Boys — J, in particular — ahead of whatever this witch wants to do."

"Sounds like a good excuse, but Drummond's got it right. If we don't stop her now, we'll have a worse problem later. A problem that will threaten the boys in far more serious ways."

Drummond winked. "Thanks for the support. My question is — where do we start? I can go check Getty's grave, but I doubt we'll find his bones there. And it was tough enough for Madame Ti to locate Miller's bones without a grave. She needed help."

"Which means I probably can't do it on my own."

"No offense, doll. You're great, but we all have our limits."

Max said, "Then what? We're at a dead end?"

"You boys give up too easy." Sandra walked out of the bedroom and returned with her laptop. "Let me tell you what I learned today about an old dead witch named Delilah French. It might help." She tapped a few keys to bring up her notes, paused long enough to wink at Max, and began. "Delilah French. Born 1792 in Colchester, England. Died, presumably 1892 in Whitney, North Carolina. The *presumably* part is because there's no official record of her death. It's possible she died sometime before and was only discovered then. In fact, there's no official record of her birth, either. I went down the list of basic research sites that you've shown me over the last few years, but not a single one had any information on her."

"Nobody named Delilah French? Not even Delilah with a different last name? Maybe she got married and the records are under her maiden name."

Sandra angled her head to the side, raised an eyebrow, and came short of placing her hand on her hip.

Drummond said, "Please forgive our resident idiot. He's not trying to be offensive. He just doesn't like anybody doing a good job at his big thing."

"Hey," Max said. "Research is where I'm most valuable. I know plenty of little tricks to get the job done."

With sufficient grit in her tone, Sandra said, "If you want to spend the next few hours double-checking my work, if that'll make you feel better, then go right ahead. The fact that you'll be insulting my intelligence and undercutting the idea that you trust me, well, I'm sure that's worth it just so you can stroke your ego."

Max shrank back against his pillow. "How about I keep my mouth shut and listen to what you found out?"

"Partner," Drummond said, making no effort to hide his amusement, "you've finally said something smart. Sandra, please continue. We'll assume you've done everything possible to find what you know."

"That's where I was headed before Mr. Rude Husband decided to interject. See, I tried all the basic and obvious tactics as well as a few of Max's little tricks I've noticed peeking over his shoulder. While I did find a handful of girls named Delilah in Whitney, I also was able to trace them through wedding notices, local girl wins baking contest articles, obituaries, and things like that. I couldn't find any solid evidence of our witch. And had I not discovered her, I would've suggested Max take a crack at it."

"But you did find her."

"I certainly did. Since I knew I was looking for a witch, I went into the witch community. Coven directories, darknet websites offering true histories, that kind of thing. And there she was. If you're done being a jerk, my dear, I'll grant you that I got a bit of a thrill when I saw her name pop up."

Max tentatively nodded. "It is pretty exciting when you start zeroing in on something."

"In this case, the most interesting aspect of Delilah French was how uninteresting she was. She really only ever achieved middling status as a witch. However, she did gain a little sidenote as one of the few witches devoted to the study of — I think you can guess the answer."

"Inhuman spirits."

"Exactly. From all I could find, she never got far with it, though. Never fully succeeded. If she had, we'd be living in a very different world. She did attempt to create numerous spells, however, and wrote them down into a single book. I checked for it — there's an online database trying to track down where all these ancient texts are located — but it doesn't appear that anybody knows what happened to French's book."

Drummond said, "We're saying that she created a new spell that she thought might summon and control a spirit. She then used Captain Getty as part of her research. That about right?"

"We already figured that much," Max said. "What's new is the idea that Getty failed."

"Seeing as how there's four Civil War ghosts with bits of spirit stuck to them, I'm thinking Getty didn't fail at all."

Sandra said, "Sorry, Drummond, but this time, I think Max is right."

"Bite your tongue."

"The fact that not even Madame Ti can control this spirit suggests that Getty failed. Which also means French failed. That's how all of this starts. From what I've learned about inhuman spirits, screwing up the summoning of them is not like with a ghost."

Max swore. "They split?"

"I think so. If you try to summon a ghost and fail, the ghost doesn't appear. Or it does but then vanishes quickly. Goes back to the Other or wherever it's stuck floating around. But an inhuman spirit is, by definition, a completely different animal. Summoning one is dangerous enough, but to mess that up can have unpredictable results."

"Because the results are erratic or because it hasn't been done enough for the witches to know what results to expect?"

"Probably a little of both." Sandra's head turned toward the bedroom door. She walked over, actually put her ear to it, and raised her hand to keep the men quiet.

Drummond said, "I can go peek in the hall."

"And J can see you."

"Oh. Right."

Returning to the bed, Sandra closed her laptop. "Captain Getty attempted the spell and failed. The results were two-fold.

The first was part of what he wanted. He sought vengeance against Major Gee and those who had caused all this suffering. Well, if Gee got cursed, we don't know about it."

"But Private Miller and his pals did." Drummond paced across the ceiling. "Poor Getty never even knew. Miller didn't burst into flames or fall down screaming or anything. The guy got to live out his life. It was only afterword that the curse kicked in."

"That's right. But Miller didn't understand why. He felt pain and confusion, but he had no idea he had been cursed."

Max started to see where Sandra headed. "The tether. Miller thought he suffered because he couldn't find his bones. And after a century of that, much of it lost underwater, along comes Madame Ti. She shows him how to tether to somebody gifted enough to see him. Somebody like J. And she promises to help get Miller's bones back."

"Maybe. Or maybe he's tried this before with other witches but Madame Ti is the first to succeed. It's also possible that Madame Ti knew nothing about this until we brought her onboard, even if she wants to claim otherwise. But it doesn't matter. Because we did bring Miller to his bones and that's how he learned about the second result of Captain Getty's failure."

Drummond said, "Wardarit."

"Getty managed to actually summon the spirit but couldn't hold it. Wardarit split into four pieces, each one attaching to Miller and his friends. All four soldiers have been stuck here, unable to move on, probably suffering nonstop pain. For more than a century. It's all like Irene told us — the spirit just wants to be whole again. It's cursed, too. Free it from these ghosts, and it'll go back from where it came so it can be at peace. Likewise, the ghosts want to move on."

"If they haven't lost themselves yet. Ghosts that old, cursed for that long, might have gone insane."

"Great," Max said. "Now we can add insane ghosts to our list of problems."

"I'm not saying we shouldn't help them. Only that we need to be cautious. But nobody deserves a hundred years of torment

— well, almost nobody. Certainly not these ghosts who were too naïve and too influenced by the world they lived to know better. And Wardarit certainly doesn't deserve what's happened to it. Getty cursed that spirit every bit as much as the soldiers."

Sandra paused, and the way she frowned, Max could tell he wouldn't like what came next. Drummond saw it, too, because the ghost drew in closer and said, "What is it?"

She looked at them both. "There was no way Captain Getty could ever have succeeded at that spell. Asking him to do so was like asking a toddler to cook a souffle. Delilah French had to have known that."

"So why do it?"

"That's the real question, isn't it?"

"No." Max swung his legs to the floor, wincing at the sudden movement, and stood. "The only question we have to ask is this — what's right for J? I'm sorry for the soldiers and for Wardarit, but if Miller hadn't brought J into this mess, we'd never have known about any of it. I know what you two are thinking — you want to free everybody. Let Wardarit go back to inhuman spirit world or wherever and let Miller and friends move on. Sounds peaceful and wonderful. But you're forgetting that Madame Ti is out there. That she'll be pissed off at us, and she'll take it out on everyone. I saw her eyes. I saw her face. She'll make a point of focusing her wraith on J because it'll make us suffer even more."

Sandra moved toward him. "But honey —"

"No." Max inched back. "We've taken risks with J before. I know that. But this time we don't have the faintest idea what might happen. We can't put him in jeopardy like that."

"If we do nothing, if we walk away like Madame Ti wants, then J's life is still in jeopardy. All of our lives are."

"Besides," Drummond said, "you won't be able to forgive yourselves. I know how you think. This would haunt you worse than any ghost ever could."

Max stumbled towards the door. "I need a hot shower. Every part of me is aching." He stopped with his hand on the knob. "We'll find a way around all this." Feeling the shocked eyes on his back, Max headed to the bathroom.

Chapter 29

BETWEEN THE HEAVY THRUMMING IN HIS SKULL, the tight soreness in his gut, and the pressing concerns for his son, Max could not sleep. He marveled at Sandra's gentle snores. Each soft breath a sweet reminder that peace existed, that they had traversed treacherous paths before and always reached safe ground together. Well, safe-ish. He continued not to sleep.

After staring at the ceiling for an hour, he finally got out of bed, threw on a robe, and shuffled into the kitchen. Moving did not hurt as much as he had expected. He could feel the throb around his eye — a little swollen, definitely black and purple. But the rest of him, while not perfect, was shockingly functional.

He poured a glass of water and stared out the kitchen window. Nothing to see in the dark beyond a streetlight, parked cars, and other homes. Drummond's pale light slipped by. At least he always had his partner. Max went outside, tightening his robe against the chilly air, and nodded as the ghost rounded the corner.

"What are you doing up?" Drummond asked.

"I doubt I'll be sleeping well for a month. You? I know you don't sleep but what are you doing?"

"Pacing. Thinking." From under the lip of his hat, he peeked at Max. Then: "I might also have been patrolling the block. Making sure Madame Ti or Wardarit doesn't hit us with any surprises."

"Mind if I join you?"

Drummond gestured ahead. "Be my guest."

They strolled along the sidewalk. Max did, anyway. Drummond strolled along the air with his hands in his pockets and his head oscillating as he constantly scanned the area.

At length, he said, "Do you still think it's a mistake to come at this head on?"

"I think it's a mistake to provoke a powerful witch when we don't have any real leverage. It's not like there's an upside to any choice, though. Just seems that doing what Madame Ti asks, backing off and letting it go, is the lesser of two evils. At least, it is when thinking about J's longevity."

"I'm not so sure. You and Sandra have always faced things with that idea of pushing through it. It's not always easy to do, but straight through is the fastest way to get beyond a bad situation."

Max's slippers made a scuffling noise that sounded loud on the sleeping streets. "Things are different now. Maybe *push on through* doesn't apply anymore. Maybe it was never such a good idea to begin with. I mean we've been following that little nugget of philosophy our whole marriage, and it doesn't look like things have gotten a lot better for us. Our life is an act of jumping from one insane crisis to the next."

Drummond snorted a laugh. "That's the life of a paranormal investigator. You can't expect anything normal when dealing with ghosts and witches all the time."

"I think that's my point."

"Not a good one, if you ask me. You're in this life now. It's too late to go back, too late to change. You want to start a new career, that's one thing. But you can't unknow the existence of the supernatural. After all, you're taking a midnight stroll with a ghost — one that resides in your living room bookshelf."

Max chuckled. "There is that."

"Listen, I know what you're doing because you've done it before. Ever since the Sandwich Boys became more than a couple street kids working for you — once they were really your boys — you've gotten this way. You think somehow you can shield them from reality."

"It's not that. Not exactly. I mean I'd love for them not to have to know about curses and witches and all of it, but I've accepted that it's going to be that way. Like Sandra with witchcraft — I have to trust that all the people in my life who know about the real world will handle it with the strength of character they have."

Taken aback, Drummond said, "Oh. Then what's your problem?"

"All I'm asking for is a little stability. Year after year, our world is in constant turmoil. We've gone from rags to riches to rags again, we've lost offices, lost homes, and come close to losing one of our boys. Now the other one is in trouble. And then there's my mother."

"There it is," the ghost said, wagging his finger. "Everything else is the life we lead, and you know it. But your mother — that has nothing to do with magic. That's not something you have any chance at controlling."

Turning back to the house, Max said, "Maybe. But she said to me that now I have to be the one taking care of her. I'm becoming the parent in the relationship. How am I going to do anything to help her when I can barely help those under my own roof?"

Arching his head back with an exasperated sigh, Drummond gazed at the stars. "Don't you ever get tired of me pointing out that you don't listen to me? I know I do."

"What did I miss now?"

"You're not alone in this. Sandra and I care about those boys, too. Heck, I've been telling you stories about my life — I've actually talked about all that stuff. I hate it. But I thought it was the way to get through to you. If you're not going to listen, I'll be happy to go back to saying nothing about my personal feelings. I can hold back my emotions like the best of them."

"You'll have to remind me when that happens. I've yet to see it in all these years.'

Drummond locked his mouth shut but only for a handful of steps. "Look, all I'm trying to say is that I understand. All parents want to protect their kids."

"Not all."

"The ones that don't, or even turn on their kids, those are the monsters of the world. The rest of the ones who screw it up are just bad at it. But none of those categories apply to you. You and

Sandra have worked hard to create this family, and you're afraid to lose it. But not pushing through your problems, rejecting that idea which has brought your family together, well frankly, only a nincompoop would do that. It'll leave you cowering in the corner, afraid to act, afraid you might lose, just waiting for the bad things to happen. And they will. Because you won't be the one fighting back, fighting through."

Max grimaced — partly from his sore ribs, partly from knowing Drummond was right. Maybe more because Drummond was right.

"You know," Max said as they reached the driveway, "it's usually Sandra's job to give me a pep talk, turn me around when I need it."

"Don't get used to it."

"Who knows? Maybe it wasn't you at all. Maybe the simple walk in the fresh night air was what I needed to clear my head."

"Wait a minute. You're not stealing the credit I earned."

Max sauntered up to the concrete step at the kitchen door. He thought back to the few times Drummond had opened up to him. They always came along when things were serious. Dire. The kind of impending-death that confessions were made for. But this time was more about keeping Max focused on what mattered, on not letting the future dictate the present. Maybe the difference wasn't as great as he wanted it to be, but Max had this sense that their midnight stroll meant more.

Drummond took the posture of leaning against Max's car, and it came close to looking natural. Not entirely, though. "Well, partner, I'm thinking that in the morning, we'll get back on the Getty train. Try to figure out where to go next."

"No."

"What do you mean *No?* I thought we worked out all of your worrywart nonsense."

"That's not what I'm saying. You're right. Just like Sandra would say, we've got to go through this thing. But we can't wait until morning. Because here's the part you keep missing — I can't simply not worry about J. Especially because he's caught in the middle of all this. When the sun comes up, it'll be Monday, and J will go off to school. But when he gets home, he'll want to jump right back into the case."

"Ah, and you want to have it all sewn up by then."

"If it's possible. It's a short window, but we've done far more with less time. That is, assuming you'll help me."

Drummond scowled. "I'm your partner. Of course, I'm going to help. What do you need?"

"We've got to find Getty's bones before Madame Ti. But she's got a big head start on us." Max paused to think through a handful of ways to move forward. At length: "I want you to go back to the Other. Talk to everybody again. See if you can find any lead on Getty."

"What about Sandra?"

Max glanced back at the house. "Let her sleep. I won't be back until sunrise, and at least one of us should be semi-conscious for the boys and for the case."

"Sunrise? Where are you going?"

"The only place I can think of that might have a clue about Getty — his grave."

Chapter 30

LIKE MOST CEMETERIES, the Historic Salisbury National Cemetery did not put too much effort into security measures. Grave robbers still existed but not in the same way or the same numbers as they did long ago. There were far better ways to steal jewels in the modern world than trespassing into a cemetery and spending hours digging deep into the ground with the hopes of snatching a ring or a necklace. The contemporary grave robber was smarter — usually a grave digger who would take the rings after the mourners had left and before plowing all the dirt into the hole. Or, for the truly sophisticated, the robbers swiped the valuables with the help of the mortician.

These morbid thoughts rolled through Max's head as he climbed over a low stone wall. When he came the first time, he entered through the back. This time he walked right around the main building — a barn-shaped structure painted white. Streetlights from the bordering neighborhood spilled a fraction of light across the land, creating jagged shadows off the headstones.

Keeping his flashlight low to the ground to avoid drawing attention, he scurried along the orderly rows of graves. He expected most people to be asleep. However, every community had its share of insomniacs. Hopefully, nobody living nearby with a view of the cemetery qualified.

Up ahead, Max spotted the large tree. He shuddered as his eyes darted around, searching for Ruby. All his bruises flared at the thought.

He should have brought Drummond. This entire endeavor would have been easier with the ghost's eyes. But also, so much harder with his constant commentary and musings. Plus, Max needed any lead they could snag. He had meant everything he said. If J finished the school day and this case was still going strong, he would insist on helping. And that young man had proven he wouldn't accept *No,* that he could be more than stubborn. For some reason, Max thought of Sandra. He smirked.

Though all his amusement drained away as he closed in on Captain Getty's grave. Because more than ever before, Max knew that if J got involved further, Madame Ti would use him — either as leverage or for whatever depths she could mine from his gifts. He shoved off the encroaching argument that he was being paranoid. After all, Ruby had been assigned to follow J on his date. That wasn't paranoia. They were watching him.

A rumble in the distance. Another storm perhaps. Or a train closing in — the tracks paralleled the main road to the cemetery. But the wind picking up suggested a storm.

Max paused to stare at Getty's grave. Just a patch of dirt featuring white stone uniform with all the others. Sometime in the future, not too far away, he would stand before another patch of dirt with a headstone — his mother's.

Did she even want to be buried? Maybe she preferred cremation? He supposed such instructions would be in her will, but then he had to question if she had even put together her will.

The beam from his flashlight bounced about, and he had to push his shaking hand against his thigh in order to stop it. Handling his mother's affairs, dealing with the thought of losing her, preparing to aid her in these final years — that was all for another day. Tonight had to be about the case. About J.

With careful motions and slow breaths, Max regained his composure. He inspected the area around the grave. A line of dead grass formed a circle — leftovers from Madame Ti's attempted spell. Undisturbed ground otherwise.

His skin prickled, starting at the nape of his neck and spreading across his body. A ghost passing too close. Not unexpected in any cemetery but more often the experience in a military cemetery. A lot of unnatural deaths haunted these places. War does that.

Squatting to the side of the grave, Max ran his flashlight up and down the grass. Madame Ti had said the bones were missing, and he believed her, but whoever took them had to have done so long ago. If more recent, then the culprit would have had to replace the chewed-up grass with fresh sod. No matter how good they were at blending it in, Max should still have been able to notice the seam. Not everywhere, but at least in one spot somewhere. Yet still the ground looked untouched.

Another swish of icy air covered his skin. He gazed across the empty cemetery. "I know it's crowded in here, boys, but let me do what I have to and I'll leave you alone."

Returning to the work at hand, Max examined the headstone. He took extra care to watch where he stepped — in case he had annoyed one the neighboring ghosts by stepping on the dead man's grave. Captain Getty's headstone looked like all the others. The inscription followed a standard format — a cross engraved at the top followed by:

CPT ARNOLD P. GETTY
US ARMY

The next two lines — the dates for birth and death — had been worn away while the words ALWAYS IN OUR HEARTS remained clear on the bottom. Odd. Erosion did not tend to be so specific. Perhaps the erasure of the dates was a byproduct of Madame Ti's spell.

Max stepped around to the back of the headstone. He saw it right away. Under daylight, the markings would have blended in with the stone or looked like scuffs. But under the harsh beam of his flashlight and the deep shadows that formed in the dark, Max saw the swirling lines crossing with a jagged sigil. The remnants of a spell.

Without a phone, he couldn't take a picture, so he pulled out a small notebook and started drawing. But another cold touch passed through him — hard enough to jolt his hand and ruin the sketch. He tried to erase the mistake and fix it, but years of experience being married to a witch told him these things needed to be as exact as possible.

He started again. Less than two lines drawn and a solid punch of ice slammed into his side. He rolled onto the grass, clutching his ribs.

A small chill, he could handle, but an outright attack — how was that possible? Max checked his pocket. Sandra's ward was still there. Why hadn't it worked? Even as he thought the question, the answer barreled into him.

Madame Ti.

When she and Ruby had interrogated him, she cast a spell that fizzled out. The ward had protected him then. But like many wards, they break when assaulted by a strong enough spell. The piece in Max's pocket was useless now.

"Okay," he said, struggling to his feet while trying to stay out of any ghost's personal space. "I got the message. You want me gone. I'm trying to help my son, though."

Another icy touch — one that didn't stop until Max jumped forward, out of the ghost's reach. Apparently, the sympathy approach wasn't going to work. He expected the attack to follow but the ghost must have peeled off.

"I will leave. I promise. But Captain Getty's bones have been taken away, and I want to find them. Help put him to rest."

The world hung in cold silence. Max waited for a judgement, and when no further assaults occurred, he decided that must have meant they would allow him to finish the sketch. A short sigh scratched at his lungs, confirming that a ghost had hurt him more than a simple warning. Edging back toward the headstone, Max lifted his pencil, readjusted the flashlight on the etching, and started to draw.

He never got more than a line done when an ice block of air smashed his leg out from under him. The pain a ghost endures when touching the real world was intense, yet they pummeled him like a street gang committing a late-night mugging. Max covered his head and pulled his legs up. He screamed. Frosty brick after frosty brick plowed into his back, his arms, his legs.

When the cold hits finally stopped, he rolled back, grabbing the flashlight on the way. Staggering to his feet, he weaved and wobbled toward the main road. His breaths were short. His eyes unfocused. Whenever he slowed, a chilling wind blew at his back, though the storm winds came from the front.

They were taunting him. Shoving him in the back like school bullies following their target down the hallway. He stumbled forward, the cold doing more to numb the pain than he wanted to admit. Not for the first time, Max felt gratitude that he could not see all ghosts. He had no desire to witness the twisted anger from those abusing him. He had no desire to see the onlookers, the ghosts who even in death refused to help someone in need.

At the stone wall bordering the exit, Max flopped over and crumpled on the other side. Safe. Any ghost that angry and existing in a cemetery would not have the ability to leave. They were either cursed to this place, tethered to their bones, or lost in the confusion of how they died. Whatever the case, they were not free to follow. Not unless a witch ...

Madame Ti.

She must have done something to these ghosts. Made a deal with them or cursed them further or simply threatened them. She knew he might come back. Had to know. So, she set this unwelcome greeting.

At least, they hadn't attacked him again. She could have set them free. Except if she had, they would never have stuck around to attack her prey.

Back on his feet, he managed to reach his car, no doubt looking as if he had downed a fifth on his own.

"What happened to you?" Drummond said as he appeared at Max's side.

"A couple of your friends decide to throw me an ice party."

Drummond snatched a quick look across the cemetery. "You want me to go straighten them out?"

"Not unless they give you trouble."

"Why would they do that?"

"Because I want you to go in there, go to Getty's grave, and look at the back of it. Madame Ti must have put some kind of whammy on the headstone as a trigger. Every time I tried to draw the symbol on the back, those ghosts attacked. Once they started, they wouldn't stop."

"I'm not much of an artist, and the pain to take the time to copy the symbol would make it near impossible to actually do anything."

"I just want you to look at it. See what it is. Sandra will need us to provide some reference to it, and I shouldn't be the only source."

Drummond glanced at the cemetery again and tapped his chin. "Before I go fighting a cemetery full of angry, anguished ex-soldiers, let me take a stab at what this symbol looks like. I'm guessing it has some swirling lines up top like wind blowing, and below you saw a bunch of jagged lines like shark teeth. Sound about right?"

"Yeah. Too right." Max opened the door and fell into the driver's seat. "How did you know all that?"

As Drummond drifted through the car to the passenger side, he said, "Because I had a very profitable trip to the Other this time."

Max tried to grin. When that failed, he reclined the seat all the way back and closed his eyes. "Tell me while I rest. And if I fall asleep —"

"You won't. Not with what I learned."

"Then I'm giving you as much attention as I have to spare."

With a grunt, Drummond said, "Rest up and listen. I went to the Other, and wouldn't you know it, now that Miller's back with his bones, everybody suddenly has loose lips. Of course, I started asking around but I also got to thinking."

"Uh-oh. That's not good."

"You want to wisecrack or you want to hear this? I'm not the one who almost turned into cold storage."

Max grinned and thought he heard a soft chuckle from his partner. "Sorry. Please, continue. You were telling me that you were thinking."

"Yeah, I was wondering why the ghosts were willing to talk when Miller still was stuck, just in a different way."

Sitting up until the pain brought him back down, Max said, "That's actually a good question."

"I know. I called on a few of my better contacts, and from

what they said, seems that the ghosts are more afraid of attracting a witch's attention than a spirit's. I pointed out that the spirit was brought into this by a witch but that didn't matter to them. One said to me that no witch could ever really control a spirit or even summon a spirit and that if I was telling the truth, then it was just dumb luck."

"You think they were all afraid of Madame Ti? They figured she cursed Miller?"

"Not quite. See, the more I looked into it, the more I found that there were a few witches involved in all this. Delilah French started it, but the ghosts of the Other don't fear her. Madame Ti, on the other hand, has actual reach in the Other. There are ghosts that will carry out her orders for fear of what she might do to them or their loved ones."

"Like a Mafia don still running things from inside prison."

"Pretty close."

"Then the ghosts knew Madame Ti was trying to use Miller."

"Right. They didn't care why. They just weren't going to help us get in the way of whatever that witch wanted. But now that she's done with Miller — at least, as far as the Other is concerned — the fear is lifted. For now."

"Hold on." Max sat up and readjusted the seat. "You just said a *few* witches were part of the Miller case. Other than Madame Ti and Delilah French, who else is there?"

"Told you there'd be no sleeping. Anyway, it kept bothering me that there's this direct line from Delilah French to Madame Ti through this one ghost, this one spell. And the inhuman spirit, too — can't forget that."

"Why is that a problem? There's got to be tons of curses out there that are decades old, doing nothing but waiting. Each one is a direct line from the witch that cast it to the witch that stumbles upon it."

"True, true. But the difference here is Wardarit. An inhuman spirit represents a lot of power. The idea that French tricked Miller into summoning the thing and then walked away from it all seems ridiculous. The idea that knowledge of this inhuman spirit would lay dormant until Madame Ti came onto the scene is downright laughable. That got me looking for a stronger link between the two witches."

"Are you telling me you actually hit the books and did some research?"

"Like you? Never. I did what any self-respecting dead gumshoe would do — hit the pavement and ask questions. I started by paying a visit to Blinky DiMotta. In life, he was a two-bit pool hustler who always had an ear to the ground in Chicago. In death, not much changed. There's no money in the Other, no real hustle to be had, but Blinky traded in information, so it made sense to talk with him first."

"Anybody named Blinky is bound to be your first choice of informant."

"Laugh all you want, but that bum pulls through with real solid leads every time. He didn't fail me this time, either. Like all the ghosts in the Other, Blinky knew about Miller and to keep quiet unless he wanted to feel the wrath of Madame Ti. Now that he could talk on it, he told me that nobody knew what it was all about. The word was to say nothing regarding Miller, and that's it. No explanation as to why, and ghosts don't really care too much about the games living people play. However, Blinky gave me the name of a ghost that might have something to help — Wally Stokes."

"Should I know him?"

"Not at all. Like Delilah French, he lived an average life and never achieved anything special or noteworthy. But, also like Delilah French, he explored witchcraft. Wally was determined to become the first male Madame. That never happened. Blinky sent me to him because Wally lived in North Carolina around the same time as French. When I talked with him, Wally told me that while he never met the witch, he knew of her, and more importantly, he knew Angela Setter."

"And should I know her?"

"No. Stop asking that."

"You keep saying these names like they mean something."

"Just close your mouth and listen. Angela Setter worked for Delilah French as the witch's assistant. When I met with her, she was thrilled to talk with me. French was no longer around, had moved on decades ago, so when all this happened with Miller, Angela had nobody to tell about it. After all these years, French was vindicated. Miller's case was proof that French knew what she was doing, wasn't a crackpot. Then she said that at least Deloris could revel in all of this."

Max kept silent.

"You can ask about that name."

"I've got more parts of my body aching than not, so please, get on with it."

Shaking his head, Drummond said, "You have no flare. Anyway, the point of who Deloris was is the point of where we went wrong. See, we kept looking at how French used Getty to experiment her spell, and how Getty screwed it up which led to Miller and friends being cursed. But we were asking the wrong question."

"We've been asking a lot of questions about French, Getty, and Miller. Which one didn't we ask?"

Drummond lifted his head as if having his portrait painted by a famous artist. "What did Getty have to pay in his deal with French?"

Max's entire body seemed to be gaping in disbelief. "You don't mean it? Deloris?"

"According to French's assistant, Angela, the deal the witch made with Getty was the spell for a child. During the time she taught Getty all the intricacies of summoning an inhuman spirit, they slept together until she became pregnant."

"All of this to have a child?"

"More than that. She wanted a specific child — a girl to raise into a witch that would continue her work. French knew that even with the aid of witchcraft, she would never live long enough to see her own success. But with an heir, the study of spirits could continue, and if not her child, then perhaps her child's child would learn how to control all that power."

Max's gut clenched. "Are you saying that Madame Ti is Delilah French's descendant?"

"Thankfully, no. If that were true, then Madame Ti wouldn't

have had to go through all this with Miller. She'd have known all about Getty from the start. For that matter, she would've had Getty's bones in her possession for years now."

"Well, we know that nobody has succeeded with French's spells because nothing crazy bad has happened. If Deloris had figured it out, she'd probably still be alive and might have reshaped the world so that she was President of the United States or something."

Drummond raised his eyebrows. "Witches can be brazen, but not like that. They prefer to control the world from the shadows. It's a lot easier when you don't have to worry about PR. But you're not too far off. The way I see it, Deloris worked side by side with her mother throughout their lives. We know Delilah lived to be a hundred years old, so they had a lot of time together. After Delilah died, Deloris continued on. Probably redoubled her efforts out of grief."

"You think it was Deloris. Her mother died in 1892. By that point, the Civil War was long over and Captain Getty dead and buried. Deloris would have no trouble sneaking into the cemetery one night and digging up Getty's bones. She then scratches in her mother's symbol and her own because Getty's her father and family is family no matter what."

"Right. Then Deloris works with those bones to gain control of Wardarit but she fails. Maybe even enlists her own daughter to continue — if she had one. I haven't had time to work that out."

Max said, "It doesn't matter. Deloris or another in the family line had to have taken it from there. Realized how powerful those bones could be. That witch did not want any other witch to be able to finish Delilah's work."

"Or perhaps she wanted the work finished but only with the French name attached. I think she hid the bones so people like Madame Ti couldn't get to them."

"Possibly. It doesn't matter, though," Max said, starting the car, "because I've got a good idea that there's only one place this particular witch daughter would want her father's bones to go — Graveyard Island."

Chapter 31

MAX SPENT THE FIRST HALF of the drive down to Whitney arguing with Drummond. The ghost was well-intentioned, trying to persuade him to go home first, wait until the Sandwich Boys went off to school, and then take Sandra along. While Max agreed that having Sandra at his side would be a great asset, the time factor stopped him. If he waited like Drummond suggested, they would be hitting upon two o'clock in the afternoon by the time they reached the island. The boys would be home long before Max and Sandra returned, and that would engage a series of questions, the answer of which would serve to confuse PB and fail to satisfy J. The case would most likely not be over, and they'd have to return to the island the next day. J would insist on coming.

"Besides," Max said, "you were the one advocating that I return to the ol' *push on through* philosophy. That's what I'm doing."

That got the ghost quiet for a bit. Long enough for Max to point out that without a cell phone, he could not call Sandra and explain anything. He needed Drummond to wait until the boys had left for school, then inform Sandra what they had learned and what Max had done.

"Oh, I see," Drummond said. "You want me to deliver the bad news and face her scorn."

"You do have one big advantage over me."

"Yeah? What's that?"

"She can't kill you."

Once Drummond left — grumbling even as he disappeared — Max still had half the drive to go. Normally, he would relish the quiet, the peaceful chance to ponder, the open late-night road, and the unique whisper in the air that came with it. But this time lacked all those qualities. This time, he thought of J and Miller, Sandra and Delilah, his mother and Madame Ti, Drummond and Ruby. And whenever he managed to clear his mind of the worries that lay ahead, his body reminded him of the dull bruises that ached with every motion.

His mind swirled from one face to the next. He was not thinking straight. He knew that. The panic pounding his heart told him as much. But all rational choices evaded him, lost in the wake of his certainty that any delay put J in peril.

He made a promise in that car — should he survive, he would do better. He would work hard to find some way for J to get involved without getting killed. He would work with Sandra to ease their son into this world, and give him the tools he needed to handle it. He'd do the job of any parent — just one that knows the greater truths of witches, ghosts, and magic.

When he finally reached Whitney, the horizon had lightened. Dawn would crest the trees soon. He drove along the still roads, taking the curves slow — didn't want to attract attention from those waking up.

At the railroad tracks, he pulled off and parked. From the trunk, he grabbed the tool bag, three bottles of water, and an empty, tan canvas bag. He patted his coat pocket — 9mm still there. Still empty, but he had it nonetheless.

He thought about the glove compartment — where he kept the bullets. He stood there, staring at the open trunk and thinking about loading his gun. No. Most gun-related accidents involved gun owners shooting themselves in one dumb way or another.

Promise #2 — if he survived this, he would get back to the shooting range. Practice until he truly knew what he was doing.

Closing the trunk, he turned to the tracks. Already his throat felt dry, but he resisted the urge to take a gulp of water. He would drink plenty of it later when he really needed it. For the moment, he trudged over to the rails and started hiking.

The long, straight journey promised to be tough no matter the situation, but in this case, each misplaced step jarred through all his wounds and into his bones. Little stumbles on loose rocks tore at his muscles. His deeper breathing scratched at his lungs and his sweat stung every nick along his skin.

"I'm pretty messed up," he said and laughed. At least he still had a sense of humor. Maybe his body wasn't so bad after all. If he could joke about it, perhaps his state of mind only made his injuries seem dire. "I guess I'll find out when I either reach the island or fall over dead."

Thinking of death brought to mind ghosts, and those two ideas shifted toward his mother. Because back when he had considered telling PB about the paranormal, about the possibility of Max's mother being a ghost, it felt abstract. It mostly still did. But somewhere inside him, the inevitable could not be denied. And the idea of his mother tagging along his life forever terrified him. She could quite literally drive him crazy.

He found that so strange — that he could love a person who makes him nuts at the same time. Perhaps PB and J felt the same way about him. To them, he might be this guy who acts way too protective when they've had harder knocks than he ever did. Max didn't want to develop a love-hate relationship with them. It was bad enough with his mother. He couldn't stomach it with the Sandwich Boys.

Promise #3 — if he survived this day, he would help the boys deal with his mother's condition, and more importantly, he would do all he could not to stand in their way. Rather, he would help them find their path. If that meant helping J become a detective of the paranormal, then so be it.

The rest of his hike progressed in a blur of step after step with the occasional break for a glug of water. Whenever his mind drifted, he pushed aside the treacherous thoughts and returned to his family. They would be his strength.

When he finally reached the first set of gravestones, the sun had finished blasting the sky with pink and orange. The strong blue of a clear day spread out above, but none of that spectacle eased Max. He trudged on ahead, steeling against possible attack — natural or paranormal. He kept his pace, even and constant, until he stood before the grave of Delilah French.

"Where else would a daughter want her father's bones to be buried but right with her mother?" He paused as if waiting for a reply. Then he dropped the tool bag and pulled out a small shovel.

From the first breaking of ground, Max knew he was in for an arduous day. North Carolina clay was unforgiving — dense, tough, and heavy. Add to that his beaten body and each shovelful promised that the next might break him in two.

But he pushed on.

Any moment he considered quitting — and there were plenty — he thought of J, Sandra, PB, and his mother. He even thought of Drummond a few times. When the pain riding his spine or the fire biting his muscles threatened to stop him from digging another inch, he remembered that he wasn't the only one searching for these bones. Eventually, either through hard research or hard witchcraft, Madame Ti would figure out the truth. If he stopped now, she would finish the job, take control of Wardarit, and nothing about the witch community would be the same.

He only allowed himself two breaks to stretch his back, guzzle water, and catch his breath. Yet even those short five-minute respites gave him a terrible sense of losing ground as if he ran a sprint and Madame Ti was closing in. More likely Ruby — with blue hair and racing stripes painted on her cheeks.

Max chuckled as he plunged the shovel in one more time. He hit something hard. Not the wood of a coffin. Might have been a large rock — he had certainly dug out quite a few — but it lacked a similar sound as before. With quick, short digs, he revealed a flash of white. Bone white.

Finding renewed energy from depths he did not know he possessed, he made rapid work of uncovering Captain Arnold Getty. The bones had been set in a small pile atop Delilah French's coffin, and Max took great care in removing each piece. He handled them like precious artifacts, lifting them one by one out of the grave and placing them in the empty, tan canvas bag.

An adult human body contained two hundred and six bones. Max knew he had come nowhere close to moving that many.

Not even half as much. As he raised the final one — Getty's skull — he wondered how many times Deloris had used some of her father's bones in an attempt to gain control of the inhuman spirit. Burning away bone after bone until only these few remained.

She must have toiled for years at it. Afraid to use the most important ones — like the skull — because they belonged to her father and because she wanted to have something substantial to bury with her mother. Yet the same obsession that drove Delilah French plagued the daughter. After all, she destroyed over a hundred bones trying to create and master a single spell. That was beyond determination. In Max's opinion, that was madness.

After crawling out of the grave, he set the skull atop the bone pile and zipped the bag shut. He heard the cocking of a handgun. Too tired to snap into action, he raised his head and offered an exhausted grin at Ruby — that vicious, slicked-back version of her.

Stepping out from behind, Madame Ti peered down the hole in the ground. "Well," she said, picking up the canvas bag. "Here we are again."

Chapter 32

SIGNALING WITH HER GUN, Ruby forced Max back into the open grave. Her nose wrinkled and her lip snarled as if she smelled something foul.

Max sat on the edge of the grave and eased down. "I'm sorry, but I have to be honest — black-haired Ruby is one of my least favorite."

"Shut up before I shoot you in the leg."

Madame Ti said, "Now, now, we've talked about this. You need to control yourself."

Gazing up, feeling the cold walls on either side, Max said, "Why are you doing this to me? You won. You've got the bones. Wardarit will be yours eventually. Hurting me now won't change that."

"True. Though an inhuman spirit does feed off negative energy, and I can't think of anything more negative at the moment than your current state."

Ruby said, "A bullet in him would heighten that negative energy a lot."

"I suppose so." Madame Ti patted Ruby's shoulder. "However, I need him alive for a bit longer. Also, while pain does create the energy Wardarit will enjoy, there are far deeper ways to hurt someone, to bring out their true anger and hatred. That's the filet mignon for a spirit."

Leaning his back against the dirt, making a show of being calm and casual, Max said, "Well, if I've got to be a meal, at least I'm top of the line."

"Ah, there's that so-called wit of yours. I don't think you'll be so full of mirth when you understand how helpless you've been this entire time."

"I'm sure you're going to gloat and tell me even if I begged you not to, so you might as well get on with it. I'd like to get home for lunch."

Madame Ti's mouth twitched. "I am the reason you are standing in that grave. When I learned about Private Miller, I provoked him to seek out young J. And, yes, I did so because I knew that would bring you and your wife to my door. I wanted your help to find Captain Getty's bones, and I doubted you would ever help me were I honest about it."

"You got that right." Max chuckled. "Is this it? This is your big plan to get me angry and feed your pet spirit? Because we already considered this and, frankly, I don't believe a word you've said. Maybe you needed Sandra's help casting a spell — though any witch would probably do — and maybe you needed my help to find out about Getty and lead you to this grave — but a few spells or some well-spent research time would have done that for you."

"I think you underestimate how good the Porter Agency is at finding things. And while other witches could have helped me, your wife has proven to be quite intuitive and very creative with her spellwork. She's going to be quite formidable one day."

"Wow, compliments." Max grinned. "You sure know how to wring the anger out of me."

"Unfortunately, it's true. When this all started, I only knew of rumors about Private Miller. I used a spell to bring him to me, and that only confirmed that he was cursed. The rest of the story was questionable."

His grin faltered. "That's why you threatened everyone in the Other. If we found out everything right away, we might not have helped Miller because we wouldn't want to help you."

"That's why I used J. It guaranteed the outcome I sought."

"No. Still not buying into it. There's no possible way you could know that we'd come to you. We almost didn't. What if Sandra's creative intuition came up with an idea that solved it without you?"

Madame Ti gestured toward Ruby. "I had her following you all the time. Whether you worked with me or not, you were going to lead me here eventually. Having you come to me made it easier, especially in finding Getty's grave, and best of all, it brought the bonus of you making a witch's deal."

Max's body slouched as he hung his head. He could dismiss all of her statements but one — Ruby. He thought back to those moments in the last several days when his instincts warned him that somebody watched from afar, when he felt the presence of another in the distance, when he swore something other than a ghost tracked his movements. Now he knew. Ruby had been there all along, shadowing every step they made. Waiting. If any part of him still doubted, gazing into her arrogant eyes confirmed it all.

Bending down to caress the canvas bag, Madame Ti said, "The trouble I've gone through to get these. Yet I must admit, Mr. Porter, that you've been a bit of a disappointment. Until now, I haven't had to deal with you directly apart from our first meeting during the Mobley-Magi conflict. I was impressed with the Porter Agency then. That's why I thought you would be perfect for this project of mine."

"You got what you wanted," Max said, each word bitter and disgusted. "I should think you owe us a bonus — or at least basic payment for services rendered would be nice."

"I suppose. After all, here we are with the bones I sought. And yet, I expected more of a challenge. You made it all too easy."

"Then tell me this — why did you —"

"No. No more." When she stood, she held one of Getty's bones in her hand — a tibia, Max thought. She looked down into the grave, and her eyes flared — gone was all sense of the person beyond the witch. "We have work still to do."

Ruby widened her stance and steadied her weapon with both hands. "Finally. At least he's already in a grave. It's convenient."

"No, child, you have to wait."

"Then what are we going to do with him? You can't let him go."

Raising the bone, Madame Ti said, "We have to test my spell. We might have to test it many, many times."

Chapter 33

PACING UP AND DOWN the short length of the grave, Max rattled his brain for an idea — any idea — that might get him out of this. But nothing came. Except a few choice words for being hot-headed and rash.

A short distance away, Madame Ti could be heard reciting her spell. Ruby stood firm at the grave's edge, keeping her handgun trained on him. When he paced to one end, the handgun followed. When he paced to the other, the handgun followed. And Madame Ti continued her spell.

At one point, two purple shapes floated overhead like low-lying clouds. Though Max could not see the other two, he had no difficulty picturing all four parts of Wardarit drifting closer and closer to Madame Ti's casting circle. They were drawn to her spell like sailors heeding a Siren's call.

Flashes of sharp light burst behind Ruby, and Madame Ti's voice deepened and grew hoarse. Max stood still and watched in the direction of all this activity. He expected, hoped, that Ruby would take a peek. She could see the dazzling light show reflected on the trees surrounding them. Any person's curiosity would urge them to glance back, and that short glance would give him an opening. But she never wavered.

"The bonds are broken," Madame Ti bellowed despite the obvious strain on her voice. "That which was imprisoned is now free. That which has been held down is unleashed. And I call upon you, now, inhuman spirit Wardarit, to grant me your aid as I have aided you."

The flashes of light brightened even as the color darkened — from bright yellow to a dark plum. Ruby let out a soft grunt, something akin to a chuckle, and lowered her weapon. Then she turned and strolled away. Nothing could have terrified Max more. If she thought that Madame Ti's magic no longer required her to hold a gun on Max, then Madame Ti's magic must have worked. Or come close enough to matter.

Despite his spiraling thoughts, it occurred to Max that by walking away, Ruby allowed him to leave. He grabbed the top edge of the grave and pulled up. But as his head broke the surface, he saw Wardarit hovering in the casting circle — a massive ball of purple swirling color. Madame Ti stood outside the circle with her hands out as if she held this ball — a giant beach ball of venom and fury. She clapped her hands closed, and as Max tried to get one foot over the edge, the inhuman spirit shot toward him.

Max flinched at the sudden charge, lost his grip and fell back into the open grave. The air whooshed out of him. As he struggled for a breath, the purple ball appeared above. It broke into four pieces, audibly snapping like timber crashing down.

One of the four sprang at Max. Though he batted at the thing, it evaded his weakened blows like a trained boxer, weaving under and nailing Max in the chest. He coughed and wheezed. Two more sections of the spirit reached down and looped around his arms. They hauled him out of the grave and slammed him onto the ground.

Clenching his face tight as groans seeped between his lips, Max tried to roll up to his knees. Before he could get one leg under, all four parts of Wardarit converged around him. Halfway up, his muscles screaming up his spine, Max concentrated on curling his fingers into a fist.

But as the spirit hovered, memories of being entered, being possessed, being pushed toward madness by an inhuman spirit flooded through him. His stomach curdled, and he tumbled to the side as his abdominal muscles constricted in a useless attempt to purge him from this evil. Tears tickled his cheeks. He knew what was coming. He knew he couldn't stop it. And he had no assurance that he could fight it off this time.

Except the spirit did not plunge into him. Its four pieces moved in slowly. With swagger. Like bullies who knew the time to destroy their target neared, and they couldn't wait to get started.

"Aw, come on," Max said, hating the tearful whine he heard. "Don't listen to that witch. She's using you. I got the bones for you. Without my help, she never would have found the way to free you."

One part of Wardarit dashed by Max, slapping through him like a bag of stones. He flailed onto his back, clutching the shoulder which took the brunt of the abuse. He screamed.

"You can break free from her. Go home and be wherever you like. She's not strong enough to stop you."

From near the casting circle, Madame Ti said, "You're pleading will only encourage it more."

"Really?" Ruby said. "Then keep pleading. Beg for your life."

Max couldn't tell where Ruby now stood, but from the tone in her voice, he knew she had changed her hair. That odd thought popped into his head at the same time another piece of spirit popped him in the jaw. He arched back and ended flat on the ground.

"Miller!" Max's voice cracked. "I helped you. I got your bones back, buried them, set you free from your curse. Your friends, too. Please, help me."

"So sorry, Mr. Porter," Madame Ti said. "Miller and his fellow soldiers have happily moved on. There will be no saving you today."

Max lifted his head to stare at her, wishing his eyes could pierce through her heart. Or at least knock Getty's bones out of her hands.

The bones?

She clutched them tight, weaving them through the air like a symphony conductor. The spell must connect the bones and her control over the spirit. Max pushed onto all fours. All he had to do was get those bones away from her.

The spirit whacked his backside like a principal paddling a student. The purple lights flashed and Max suspected the spirit was laughing.

He knew what he wanted to do, but it would never happen

unless she called off that creature long enough for him to muster his strength. Just a little time. Enough that he could lunge once. That's all. He had no delusion that he would get more than that.

"Wait, wait," he said, waving one hand as he pressed upright. "You've got to stop. If you don't, you'll end up killing me."

"That's pretty much the idea."

"If you do that, then I won't be around to fulfill my part of our deal." He raised one foot and planted it firm on the ground. "I know I haven't been at my best with this case. I probably should've seen what you were up to, but your enthusiasm here is getting the better of you."

She motioned with the bone, and he could feel the spirit rushing towards him.

"You need me to fight the Hulls," he spit out. She pulled back, and Wardarit whipped by without striking him. "You do. You know it. That's why you made the deal. You can get plenty of witches to give you power, but none of them have her trust. Cecily Hull trusts me."

"I doubt that."

"More than she trusts you." With a long moan, he pressed down until he stood on both feet. "You need me to get close to her. Because when you strike — and we both know you will strike at her eventually — you're going to need that advantage. She can't see it coming, and the time it takes to cast any significant spell will be too long. That's why you really wanted to deal with me." He staggered forward a few steps. Close enough as long as she didn't move away. "Obviously, the rest of this — the bones, the spirit, the spells — that was all icing. After all, I might call you crazy, but you'd never bet all of your future on the idea of succeeding with a spirit spell. Not when so many witches before have failed."

Madame Ti jutted her chin at him. "Yet here I am, holding these bones, in complete control of an inhuman spirit."

"I wouldn't say complete."

Max lunged at her, scrambling to knock the bones from her hands. The shock on her face propelled him further, faster. Even if she shifted away causing him to miss the bones, he decided in that fraction of second that he would tackle the woman. Let her feel the hard ground slam all the air from her lungs. She would most likely drop the bones, and they could scrap for them after.

But it never happened.

After the initial few steps, Ruby intervened. She clocked him on the side of the head — with her fist? the butt of her weapon? — and down he went. As his brain tried to recompose the moment, put all the sounds and sights into order, he caught a flash of deep red hair and a tight fist racing towards him.

The flurry of punches came upon him so fast, he couldn't register the pain. Or perhaps, his body had endured too much and simply gave up trying. He knew Ruby struck and struck and struck, yet his mind had separated.

As if from a far-off world, he heard Madame Ti speak. "Stop. I don't want you to kill him."

"Aw, I ain't fixin' to kill him. But I sure do want to bring him close."

"That's enough. We have Wardarit now. While I'm sure you would have more fun doing the dirty work yourself, you will always leave evidence behind. I could not, in good conscience, ask you to risk jail when an inhuman spirit will do the job, and it will never tie back to us. Today, with the death of Mr. Porter, we will send a message to all who need to hear it that we have the impunity to take the lives of those who cross us."

The weight straddling Max lifted, and he teetered to the side. Madame Ti moved the bones in her hands as if controlling a marionette, and the spirit responded. It swished across the ground until it hovered before her. She appeared to whisper something, but Max could not make it out. The world would not sit still — it kept rocking up and down as if all of Graveyard Island were a boat on a stormy sea.

Max couldn't recall ever being hit so hard in the head. He hoped he didn't have a concussion. But despite the cloudy, rolling of his mind, he comprehended enough. "Don't do this. You want to use me. I know you do."

"I would have preferred it that way, but you won't behave. Ruby saw it long ago, and now I must agree with her."

"Thank you, ma'am," Ruby said with honest appreciation.

"I've never been one afraid to admit when I make a mistake. You said from the start that I should be rid of Max Porter, and I didn't listen. But I hear you now. And so does Wardarit."

With that, the spirit circled back towards Max, elongating as it travelled at him. Like a thrown spear, it soared through the air. And Max watched it coming his way.

He always thought that at the moment of his true death, he would have that experience people often reported — seeing the important parts of their life flash before their eyes. Or perhaps snapshots of his regrets. Maybe even highlights of his happiness.

Instead, he saw the back of J's head. Instead, he heard J shouting *No!* Instead, he felt the dirt and rocks rumble as the spirit whisked around them. The air splashed with purple and a frustrated growl split like thunder.

J looked back at Max. "Don't worry. We've got you."

Just beyond, Sandra and Drummond arrived.

Chapter 34

THOUGH STILL FINDING IT DIFFICULT to keep the ground level for his spinning brain, Max could form enough clear thoughts to put things together. Wardarit, like all inhuman spirits, could not break through the shield of a person's faith. And just as Max and Sandra had deep faith in each other, J now showed that he held such faith for Max. The gentle smile they shared at that moment blazed into Max's memory as the spirit raced around them.

"Enough of this," Ruby said, stomping forward.

She raised her handgun and pointed it directly at Max's head. Then her body jittered and she collapsed — once again a victim of Drummond freezing her unconscious.

Shaking the pain off his hand, the ghost said, "I don't think I'll ever get tired of that."

"It does come in handy," Max said, trying to stand with J's help.

Madame Ti paused too long to watch what happened. When it finally hit her that neither Ruby nor Wardarit would be saving their triumph, she swiped the canvas bag with Getty's bones and ran.

Not far, though. Sandra had come prepared with a spell already held in hand, waiting for release — a useful trick for the simplest spells she had learned years ago from watching the Magi. When she let loose her attack, Madame Ti's legs gave out. The witch tumbled in the dirt.

As she attempted to stand, Max and J approached. Wardarit continued to sweep through the air around Max, but with J by his side, Max thought he'd be safe. He pulled out the empty 9mm and pointed it at Madame Ti.

"You try anything, and you'll regret it," he said.

With controlled grace, she rose to her feet. "Come now, Mr. Porter. You're no murderer. And even if you hated me enough, I doubt you would kill me in front of your son."

"True. But I have no problem putting a bullet in your leg."

Madame Ti's arrogance drifted away. For a fleeting second, she looked weak and defeated. But then she puffed up, curling her lip in disgust. "You're making an enemy of me. Not a smart move."

"Well, you know, that's my trademark." To Sandra, he added, "Dear, would you please take that bag as well as the bones in this witch's hands?"

Sandra complied, keeping a cautious eye on Madame Ti the entire time.

Drummond floated over to Max. "Take all the time you need to destroy those things, doll. J and I will make sure this spirit doesn't touch Max at all. Right, kid?"

"You know it," J said.

Sandra walked the bones back to Delilah French's grave and dropped them in. She closed her eyes and started mumbling a spell. Max peeked at her work but kept most of his focus on Madame Ti.

The witch gave an approving nod. "Smart woman. An old technique for an old spirit."

Indeed, Sandra refrained from making a casting circle or using any symbols of witchcraft. From her bag, she pulled out a box of salt and spread it over the bones. Then she squeezed lighter fluid into the grave. Finally, she picked up a fallen branch, lit it on fire, and tossed it below. The air whooped as the lighter fluid ignited. Seconds later, a rapid series of snaps like a string of firecrackers could be heard — all the bones breaking at once.

Madame Ti's head drooped. The inhuman spirit ceased its attempt to attack Max. Instead, it hovered near the witch as if debating the best vengeance to enact. But it must have decided that the human world was not worth the trouble. Wardarit vanished.

"Well, how do you like that?" Drummond said as his gaze fell around him. "You're getting a round of applause from the locals."

Max made to bow but thankfully stopped. The ghosts did not applaud him. They were impressed by Sandra.

"Please, no, it was nothing," she said, a bashful smile covering her face. "Oh, yes, we've had ghost clients many times in the past."

"As long as you can pay," Max said.

Sandra rolled her eyes, but at least she backed him up. "I'm sorry, you have to figure out a method of payment before we can look into that for you."

Drummond said, "We better finish up here or all the ghosts on this island are going to line up to hire you."

Hearing an odd scratching, Max noticed Madame Ti drawing in the dirt. "Hey. None of that." He rushed forward as she raised her hands, and he rubbed his foot across the half-drawn symbol. "If you want to get out of here in one piece, I suggest you gather your crazy friend and leave now. You try anything else, and as I understand it, there's an entire island of ghosts who want our services. They can't get our help if you're causing us problems."

"No lie on that," Drummond said. "In fact, a few of them want to give her a little nudge in the right direction."

Madame Ti shivered and looked off to her right. A shudder and she jumped back a step. Her eyes darted from one spot to the next. "Okay," she shouted. Then softer: "Okay."

Taking cautious steps, she reached Ruby. A few taps on the shoulder woke the woman. Ruby startled, but Madame Ti held her shoulders like a child waking from a nightmare. "No, no. Everything's fine. We have to leave now. We're outnumbered."

Max pointed his 9mm at Ruby. "Don't try anything stupid."

"Oh, put that toy away," Madame Ti said. "You're not going to shoot anybody. You got a win today. Congratulations."

"You don't sound all that sincere."

"I actually am — a tiny bit. Because of what you all have done, the Brotherhood can't get ahold of Wardarit, either. For that, I thank you." She took hold of Ruby's arm and the two turned away. "But don't think all is forgiven. And don't think I won't still call upon you to deliver your end of our deal."

"Wouldn't dream of it."

Max lowered his weapon as Madame Ti and Ruby shuffled off toward a small boat on the shoreline. Sandra walked up to his side and J came along the other side. He could feel Drummond behind. Nobody spoke. They stood like sentries, watching and waiting, making sure their enemy continued to retreat.

Sandra laced her fingers with Max. Then J did the same. No inhuman spirit could ever break through their wall. And if they could stand against that, Max didn't think a witch and a madwoman had a chance.

"What are you smiling at?" Sandra asked as the small motor buzzed the little boat off onto the lake.

"You saved me." Max leaned over and kissed her cheek. "Again."

"If you think a little charm is going to get you out of trouble, you're sorely mistaken. What were you thinking going off on your own?"

"I know. I do. I'm sorry."

"Don't you ever do that again."

"Don't worry." He gestured to the island. "This — I won't."

Drummond clapped his hands together. "So, kid, what do you think? Is this the life for you or what?"

They all looked to J who squirmed under their attention. With a furrowed brow, he said, "How bad do we have to worry about those two? And whatever others they get to join their gang?"

Sandra started gathering the tools. "There's always danger in the world, but I'll double the wards around the house when we get home."

"That only goes so far," Drummond said.

Max said, "Yeah, but we also have Cecily Hull on our side. She'll offer some protection if things get ugly soon."

"Not much, though. The fact of the matter is that J and his brother can't hide in the house forever. At some point, the boys have to go to school, if nothing else. That's a vulnerable location. And what about when J wants to go on a date again?"

Max picked up a shovel and handed it to J. His own muscles

couldn't handle the idea of filling in Delilah French's grave. Besides, one of the joys of parenthood was having a child labor force under your command.

As J started shoveling, Sandra said, "Drummond's right."

"I agree," Max said. Then, catching everybody's expression: "What? J's got to learn to protect himself. We can't do it forever. And who better to teach him about fighting off witchcraft than our own lovely witch?"

"Thank you." Sandra walked over and pressed Max's hand against her heart. "But he'll also need to know who his enemies truly are. Where they come from, what motivates them, and who they're related to. Any information he uncovers is vital to discovering their weaknesses. Who better than the greatest researcher I've ever known?"

Max moved in to kiss her once more when Drummond said, "You both are forgetting the most important part — J needs to know how to have fun. All this magic and death can make the world look glum all the time. Don't worry, kid. Uncle Drummond will teach you how to really enjoy life."

Though he wanted to interject, perhaps throw some caution onto Drummond's words, Max held back. One look at J stopped him. The young man filled in a grave after facing down an inhuman spirit, an insane henchwoman, and the most powerful witch in North Carolina — and he was smiling.

Sandra rested her head on Max's shoulder. "He's going to do just fine."

"I know."

Chapter 35

TWO MONTHS LATER, Max entered the Law Offices of MacGern & Brown. His mother sat in a dark-wood chair reading a copy of *Southern Living*. The walls had portraits of two staunch men from 1912 — presumably, MacGern and Brown's ancestors who founded the practice.

"Good, you're here," Mrs. Porter said as Max took the seat next to her. "I was beginning to worry."

Stationed behind an antique desk with a modern computer, a receptionist gave Max a smile of hello. He watched her for an extra second, waiting for that welcome to turn into something sinister. He couldn't help it. Even after two months of quiet, he still expected Madame Ti to come at him from some unexpected angle.

They had done all they could with spells. Sandra worked twice as hard on the house wards and made charmed pendants for the boys — difficult when the pendants also had to look cool enough to wear. Drummond patrolled the school grounds but reported no ghostly activity of any kind. And Max spent most of his time recovering.

But nothing happened.

No physical attacks. No curses or spells. No spirits. Nothing.

Sandra had to remind Max that Madame Ti did not raise Wardarit but merely attempted to control it. "That spirit was attached to Miller as part of the original curse." Max knew it, but that didn't stop him from flinching anytime he saw a flash of purple.

The longer they went without a peep from Madame Ti, the more Max's concern raised. The witch bided her time. And as the days drifted by, as they settled into their new routines, he knew that she planned something.

"Are you listening to me?" his mother said.

"Sorry."

"That's not going to cut it. I need you to be here, to listen to these lawyers. When I become too sick to handle my affairs, you're going to be the one in charge — Power of Attorney, my living will, medical decisions, and when the time comes, executor."

"I know."

"You don't. You act like you do, but I gave birth to you. I know you better than you'll ever know yourself. You think you can ignore all of this and not deal with it and then when I die — "

"Don't say that."

"It's going to happen eventually. I will die. You have to be prepared."

"I'm trying. But you're wrong."

Mrs. Porter tossed her magazine back onto the coffee table. "This is wonderful news. I must be immortal."

"I mean, you're wrong about the way I should handle all of this. You've been saying that we're going to switch roles, that I'll be the parent, but that's not true. I'm starting to see it with my own boys. I'll always be their father. What that means and how it plays is what changes."

With a roll of her eyes, she said, "What in Heaven are you talking about?"

Max paused as he tried to articulate the things tumbling around his brain. "When Sandra and I first took in PB and J, we were their guardians in every sense of the word. Our parental job was to protect them from the horrors of the world, the dangers, even from themselves. We had to make sure they ate enough, had their shots, checked their eyesight, basically do all we could to keep them alive and healthy."

"Of course. What else is a parent for?"

"But they don't need any of that anymore. They're teenagers now, and they know how to take care of themselves. We still provide those things, but they don't really require our help in basic living. No. Sandra and I have a new role as parents now."

Crossing her legs, Mrs. Porter said, "I never had to change my role. I've always been your mother and I did a fine job raising you. Why do you have to be different?"

"It's a different world. My real job now is to make sure that PB and J make it through their teen years alive, not addicted to anything, not fathers, and maybe, if I'm lucky, with some sense of direction or a goal to shoot for. The rest of it they know how to handle themselves."

"Seems that you've got it all worked out. Am I to take it, from this sudden enlightenment of yours, that you don't think you need to be the one in charge with me? Should I find some stranger to rely on for managing my affairs?"

"What? No. That's not what I'm saying at all." Max heard the rise in his voice and felt the receptionist's eyes upon him. Though still tight, he whispered, "We're not changing so that I'm suddenly parenting you. You will always be my mother and I'll always be your son. I'll always need you like that. Of course, I'm going to handle your affairs — I'm here, after all. But I don't want you to change the way you think to this fatalistic attitude you're skirting around."

"That's not what I've been doing. You really don't listen." She took a breath, and Max watched her frustration vanish like a ghost. She said, "I need to know that everything is set in place for when my end comes. Now, now, I'm not saying that I'll die tomorrow. Or even this year. I hope to live for quite a bit longer. And don't you worry about it — I'll fight to my last breath. Have you ever known me to do different?"

Max chuckled. "I guess not."

"But it's hard to face all of that if I feel that there are loose ends to deal with. You see? We go in with the lawyer today, a bit nervous, a little unsure, and we'll leave with the confidence that no matter what happens, we're prepared. I'm prepared."

Max sat back and pursed his lips. "Huh. I never saw it like that."

"Peace of mind is a big part of what I want. Knowing that whatever happens to me, I don't leave a mess for you."

He saw Ruby standing over the open grave, pointing a handgun at him, the hunger in her eye, the delight to squeeze the trigger. "Maybe I should have your lawyer set up paperwork for me, too."

"I think that's a wise decision. You never know what might happen. Car accidents, house fires, even getting hit by lightning."

"Lightning?"

"Sure, it sounds funny. Unless you're the one-in-a-million that it happens to. Then you'd feel cursed."

Max sobered fast. "Yeah. Being cursed is exactly how I'd feel."

Afterword

Hi folks! I hope you had a nice visit with the Porters. Whenever I sit down to start another one of these books, it always begins with the research. Finding those little bits of history that I can mold into a story for Max and the gang. There have been times when that research required weeks just to find an item or two that had the spark for a Max Porter book. Thankfully, this book was not like that at all. This time around, I came across everything I needed with such ease that I had to wonder if Sandra wasn't casting a spell to help me out.

It all begins with the title. I have a list of possible *Southern XXXX* titles to use or to inspire other possibilities. On the list was *Southern Graves* which had a natural fit with the series, so I thought I'd give it a spin. I googled "North Carolina graves" and the first thing that came up was Graveyard Island. I laughed. I couldn't believe this was real. And from there the ball was rolling. And rolling fast.

So, here's the stuff y'all love to know:

With the exception of Private Miller and Delilah French, all the history about Badin Lake and the creation of Graveyard Island is true. The place exists pretty much as described. I took a few liberties with the locations of some of the graves. Since we're still in COVID times at this writing, I wasn't able to drive down to Whitney and hike out there in person, so other details such as the tiny dock were fabrications. However, there is a YouTube video of some paranormal investigators walking the tracks to get to the island, so you can see for yourself what the place looks like, if you want.

Drummond's story about the Badin Bomber is also true. As is the problem of the lake being so deep and murky that divers have found it near impossible to salvage much.

While Captain Getty was my creation, the horror of Salisbury Prison was not. All the details of the prison and the doctor turned warden are true. The attempted uprising and the brutal slaughter by cannon used to quell the prisoners is also true. The two national cemeteries in Salisbury can be found easily enough, and while the prison cemetery is close to how I described it, I did need to add a few trees and stonework for the benefit of this story.

Thanks for joining me for another go around. I had a blast writing this one (I always do) and like you, I'm looking forward to see what Max and the gang get up to next.

Acknowledgements

With COVID still raging through the world (though vaccines are now being distributed, so there's hope), I have found that many of my usual writing folk who help keep me sane have been out of touch. They are other writers and editors I see at conventions, and with all conventions closed down, I miss my peers tremendously. But I've also reconnected with old friends from decades ago, and those friendships have proven to be quite strong. So, I wish to give special thanks to Maria Knapp, Cameron Francis, and Shawn Fisher for our bi-weekly Zoom chats. You guys have no clue how vital those are to keeping me going.

I also want to give big thanks to Katherine Perry for another wonderful cover. And, of course, thanks to my wife and son who continue to be the greatest joys of my life.

Most importantly, I want to thank you, my readers. Every day I sit down to write, I'm thinking of you and how fortunate I am to have your support. I'm glad my stories make you happy. Thank you.

About the Author

Stuart Jaffe is the madman behind *The Max Porter Paranormal Mysteries,* the *Nathan K* thrillers, *The Parallel Society* series, *The Malja Chronicles, The Bluesman, Founders, Real Magic,* and so much more. His unique brand of old pulp adventure mixed with a contemporary sensibility brings out the best in a variety of SF/F sub-genres. He trained in martial arts for over a decade until a knee injury ended that practice. Now, he plays lead guitar in a local blues band, *The Bootleggers,* and enjoys life on a small farm in rural North Carolina. For those who continue to keep count, the animal list is as follows: one dog, two cats, two aquatic turtles, and fifteen chickens. The horse is now at a new pasture. She's having a wonderful time hanging with a herd of thirty other horses. Much better for her. As best as he's been able to manage, Stuart has made sure that the chickens do not live in the house.

www.ingramcontent.com/pod-product-compliance
Lightning Source LLC
Chambersburg PA
CBHW030530310726
48979CB00010B/1864/J

* 9 7 8 1 9 6 3 5 1 7 0 7 1 *